JUSTINE

or

The Misfortunes of Virtue

Justine

OR

The Misfortunes of Virtue

THE MARQUIS DE SADE

WORDSWORTH CLASSICS

While the Publishers have made every effort to ensure
that the copyright in this translation is in the public domain,
they would be happy to hear
from any interested person or literary estate
that they have been unable to trace.

This edition published 1996 by
Wordsworth Editions Limited
Cumberland House, Crib Street
Ware, Hertfordshire SG12 9ET

ISBN 1 85326 635 3

Typeset by Antony Gray
Printed and bound in Great Britain by
Mackays of Chatham plc, Chatham, Kent

❦§❧

JUSTINE

or

The Misfortunes of Virtue

❦ One ❧

The triumph of philosophy would be to reveal, amply and lucidly, the means by which providence attains her ends over man; and, accordingly, it would trace those lines of conduct which might enable this unfortunate biped individual to avoid, while treading the thorny path of life, those bizarre caprices of a fate which has twenty different names, but which, as yet, has never clearly been defined.

For although we may fully respect our social conventions, and dutifully abide by the restrictions which education has imposed on us, it may unfortunately happen that through the perversity of others we encounter only the thorns of life, whilst the wicked gather nothing but roses. Things being so, is it not likely that those devoid of the resources of any firmly established virtues may well come to the conclusion suggested by such sad circumstances – that it were far better to abandon oneself to the torrent rather than resist it? Will it not be said that virtue, however fair she may be, becomes the worst cause one can espouse when she has grown so weak that she cannot struggle against vice? Will it not equally be said that, living in a century so thoroughly corrupt, the wisest course would be to follow in the steps of the majority? May we not expect some of our more educated folk to abuse the enlightenment they have acquired, saying with the angel Jesrad of *Zadig* that there is no evil which does not give birth to some good – adding that, since the imperfect constitution of our sorry world contains equal amounts of evil and of good, it is essential that its balance be maintained by the existence of equal numbers of good and wicked people. And will they not finally conclude that it is of no consequence in the general plan whether a man is good or wicked by preference; and that if misfortune persecutes virtue and prosperity almost always accompanies vice, things being equal in the sight of nature, it seems infinitely better to take one's place among the wicked, who prosper, than among the virtuous, who perish.

Therefore it is important to guard against the sophisms of a dangerous philosophy, and essential to show how examples of unfortunate virtue, presented to a corrupted soul which still retains some wholesome principles, may lead that soul back to the way of godliness just as surely as if her narrow path had been bestrewn with the most brilliant honours and the most flattering of rewards. Doubtless it is cruel to have to describe, on the one hand, a host of misfortunes overwhelming a sweet and sensitive woman who has respected virtue above all else, and – on the other – the dazzling good fortune of one who has despised it throughout her life. But if some good springs from the picture of these fatalities, should one feel remorse for having recorded them? Can one regret the writing of a book wherein the wise reader, who fruitfully studies so useful a lesson of submission to the orders of providence, may grasp something of the development of its most secret mysteries, together with the salutary warning that it is often to bring us back to our duties that heaven strikes down at our side those who best fulfil her commandments?

Such are the thoughts which caused me to take up my pen; and it is in consideration of such motives that I beg the indulgence of my readers for the untrue philosophies placed in the mouths of several of my characters, and for the sometimes rather painful situations which, for truth's sake, I am obliged to bring before his eyes.

❧ *Two* ❧

The Comtesse de Lorsange was one of those priestesses of Venus whose fortune lies in an enchanting figure, supported by considerable misconduct and trickery, and whose titles, however pompous they may be, are never found save in the archives of Cythera, forged by the impertinence which assures them, and upheld by the stupid credulity of those who accept them. Brunette, vivacious, attractively made, she had amazingly expressive dark eyes, was gifted with wit, and possessed, above all, that fashionable cynicism which adds another dash of spice to the passions, and which makes infinitely more tempting the woman in whom it is suspected. She had, moreover, received the best possible education. Daughter of a very rich merchant of the rue Saint-Honoré, she had been brought up, with a sister three years younger than herself, in one of the best convents in Paris; where, until she was fifteen years old, nothing in the way of good counsel, no good teacher, worthwhile book, or training in any desirable accomplishment, had been refused her. Nevertheless, at that age when such events are most fatal to the virtue of a young girl, she found herself deprived of everything in a single day. A shocking bankruptcy plunged her father into such a cruel situation that all he could do to escape the most sinister of circumstances was to fly speedily to England, leaving his daughters in the care of a wife who died of grief within eight days of his departure. One or two of their few remaining relatives deliberated on the fate of the girls, but as all that was left to them totalled a mere hundred crowns each, it was decided to give them their due, show them the door, and leave them mistresses of their own actions.

Madame de Lorsange, who at that time was known as Juliette, and whose wit and character were already almost as mature as they were when she had reached the age of thirty – which was her age at the time of our story – felt only pleasure at her freedom, and never for an instant dwelt on the cruel reverses which had broken her chains. Justine, her sister, however, just turned twelve, and of a sombre and melancholy turn of mind, was endowed with an unusual tenderness accompanied by a surprising sensitivity. In place of the polish and artfulness of

Juliette, she possessed only that candour and good faith which were to lead her into so many traps, and thus felt all the horror of her position.

This young girl's features were totally different from those of her sister. The one held just as much of artifice, flirtation, and guile, as the other did of delicacy, timidity, and the most admirable modesty. For Justine had a virginal air, great blue eyes gentle with concern, a clear dazzling complexion, a small slender body, a voice of touching softness, ivory teeth, and beautiful fair hair. These were the subtle charms of the younger sister, whose innocent grace and delicious features were so delicate and ethereal that they would escape the very brush which would depict them.

Each of the two were given twenty-four hours to leave the convent, and were left to provide for themselves, each with her hundred crowns, wherever and however they might choose. Juliette, enchanted at being her own mistress, wished for a moment to dry Justine's tears; but realising that she would not succeed, set to scolding instead of consoling her, exclaiming that such behaviour was foolish, and that girls of their age, blessed with faces like theirs, had never starved to death. She cited, as an example, the daughter of one of their neighbours who, abandoning her paternal home, was now being kept in luxury by a rich landowner, and drove her own carriage around Paris. Justine expressed horror at such a pernicious example, and she said she would rather die than emulate it. Moreover she flatly refused to share a lodging with her sister, since it was obvious that this young woman had decided to follow the abominable way of life which she had so recently praised.

Thus the two sisters separated from each other without promise of any reunion, since their intentions were found to be so different. Could Juliette, who had pretensions to becoming a great lady, ever consent to see again a little girl whose low and *virtuous* inclinations would disgrace her? And, on her side, is it likely that Justine would wish to risk her morals in the company of a perverse creature who was about to become the victim of vile lubricity and general debauchery? Each, therefore, relying on her own resources, left the convent on the following day as had been agreed.

Justine, who as a child had been fawned over by her mother's dressmaker, imagined that this woman would feel a natural sympathy for her position. She therefore sought her out, told her of her unfortunate position and, asking for work, was immediately thrown on to the street.

'Oh heaven!' cried the poor little creature, 'must it be that the first step I take in the world leads me only to further miseries . . . This

woman loved me once! Why, then, does she cast me away today? . . .
Alas, it must be because I am orphaned and poor . . . Because I have no
resources in the world, and because people are esteemed only by reason
of the help or the pleasure which others hope to receive from them.'

Reflecting thus, Justine called on her parish priest and asked his
advice. But the charitable ecclesiastic equivocally replied that it was
impossible for him to give her any alms, as the parish was already
overburdened, but that if she wished to serve him he would willingly
provide her with board and lodging. In saying this, however, he passed
his hand under her chin, and kissed her in a fashion much too worldly
for a man of the Church. Justine, who understood his intentions all too
well, quickly drew back, expressing herself as follows: 'Sir, I am asking
of you neither alms nor yet the position of a servant. I am not so far
reduced from my recent position in society as to beg two such favours;
all I ask of you is the advice of which my youth and my present
misfortune stand so much in need. Yet you would have me buy it with a
crime . . . ' The priest, insulted by this expression, opened the door and
pushed her brutally on to the street. Thus Justine, twice repulsed on
the first day of her isolation, walked into a house displaying a notice
and rented a small furnished room, paying in advance. Here, at least,
she was able to abandon herself in comfort to the grief caused not only
by her situation but by the cruelty of the few individuals with whom
her unlucky star had constrained her to have dealings.

❧ *Three* ❧

With the reader's permission we shall abandon our heroine for a while, leaving her in her obscure retreat. This will allow us to return to Juliette, whose career we will sum up as briefly as possible – indicating the means whereby, from her humble state as an orphan, she became within fifteen years a titled woman possessing an income of more than thirty thousand livres, the most magnificent jewels, two or three houses in the country as well as her residence in Paris, and – for the moment – the heart, the wealth, and the confidence of M. de Corville, a gentleman of the greatest influence, and a Counsellor of State who was about to enter the Ministry itself . . .

That her path had been thorny cannot be doubted, for it is only by the most severe and shameful of apprenticeships that such young women attain their success; and she who lies today in the bed of a prince, may still carry on her body the humiliating marks of the brutality of depraved libertines into whose hands she had once been thrown by her youth and her inexperience.

On leaving the convent, Juliette quickly went to find the woman she had once heard named by a corrupt friend from her neighbourhood, and whose address she had carefully kept. She arrived with abrupt unconcern, her bundle under her arm, her little dress in disorder, with the prettiest face in the world and the undeniable air of a schoolgirl. She told the woman her story, and begged her to protect her; just as, several years previously, she had protected her friend.

'How old are you, my child?' asked Madame du Buisson.

'In a few days time I shall be fifteen, Madame.'

'And nobody has ever . . . ?'

'Oh, no, Madame, I swear it to you!'

'Nevertheless it is not unknown for convents to harbour a chaplain, a nun, or even a schoolfriend who . . . So I must be supplied with certain proofs!'

'All that you need do is look for them, Madame . . . '

And du Buisson, fixing herself up with a pair of spectacles, and having verified the exact state of things, said to Juliette: 'Well, my

child, all you need do is stay here. But you must strictly observe my
advice, show the utmost compliance with my customs, be clean and
neat, economical and candid so far as I am concerned, courteous
towards your companions, and as dishonest and unscrupulous as you
like with men. Then, a few years from now, you will be in a position to
retire to a nicely furnished place of your own, with a servant, and such
proficiency in the art you will have acquired in my establishment that
you will have the means quickly to satisfy each and every desire you
may wish.'

With these words la du Buisson seized Juliette's little bundle,
enquiring, at the same time, if she were absolutely without money. And
Juliette having too frankly admitted that she had a hundred crowns, her
new-found mama quickly took possession of them, assuring her young
pupil that she would invest this small sum to her profit, and that it was
unnecessary for a girl to have money, especially as it could be a means
towards the indulgence of wickedness. Moreover, in such a corrupt
century, any wise and highly-born young lady must carefully avoid
anything which might cause her to fall into a trap. This sermon
completed, the newcomer was introduced to her companions, taken to
her room in the house, and from the following day her first-fruits were
on sale. Within four months' time the same merchandise had successively been sold to eighty different people, all of whom paid for it as
new; and it was not until the end of this thorny novitiate that Juliette
took out her patents as a lay-sister. From that moment, however, she
was readily accepted as a daughter of the house, and entered the new
novitiate of partaking in all its libidinous fatigues ... If, excepting a few
slight deviations, she had served nature during her early days in this
place, she now forgot all natural laws and began to indulge in criminal
researches, shameful pleasures, dark and crapulous orgies, scandalous
and bizarre tastes and humiliating caprices – all of which arose, on the
one hand, from a desire for pleasure without risk to health – and, on
the other, from a pernicious satiety which so wearied her imagination
that she could delight only in excess and revive herself only by way of
lubricity ...

Her morals were totally corrupted in this second school; and the
triumphs of vice which she witnessed completed the degradation of her
soul. She began to feel that she was born only for crime, and that she
might as well cultivate only wealthy and important people rather than
languish in a subordinate state wherein, though she committed the
same faults and debased herself just as much, she could not hope to
gain anything like the same profit. She was fortunate in pleasing an old
and very much debauched nobleman, whose original intention had

merely been the passing of a pleasantly salacious fifteen minutes. But she was clever enough to persuade him to keep her in magnificent style, and finally showed herself at the theatre or walking in company with the most aristocratic members of the Order of Cythera. She was admired, discussed, envied; and the roguish little cheat knew so well the art of grabbing what she wanted that within four years she had ruined three men, the poorest of whom had boasted an income of one hundred thousand crowns a year. Nothing more was necessary to establish her reputation. For the blindness of the present century is such that, the more one of these miserable creatures proves her dishonesty, the more envious men become of finding a place on her list. It would seem that the degree of her degradation and corruption becomes, in fact, the measure of those amorous feelings for her which men dare to proclaim.

Juliette had scarcely passed her twentieth year when the Comte de Lorsange, a forty-year-old nobleman from Anjou, became so infatuated by her that he determined to give her his name – not being rich enough to keep her. He allowed her an income of twelve thousand livres and assured her of the remainder of his fortune – a further eight thousand – if he died before she did. He also presented her with a house and servants, her own livery, and built up for her the kind of social importance which, within two or three years, caused people to forget the means by which she had attained such celebrity. This was the time when the wretched Juliette, forgetting all the sentiments due to her honourable birth and her excellent education, perverted by evil theories and dangerous books, anxious to be completely independent – to have a name, yet not be chained by it – began to ponder the criminal idea of shortening her husband's life . . . The odious project once conceived, she nursed it, caressed it, and finally executed it with so much secrecy that she was, unfortunately, protected against all investigation. Thus she managed to bury, together with her troublesome husband, all traces of her heinous crime.

Free once more, and still a Countess, Madame de Lorsange resumed her former habits. But, considering herself something of an important figure in society, she maintained an outward appearance of decency. She was no longer a kept woman but a rich widow who gave delightful suppers to which the townspeople and the court were only too happy to be admitted. She was, we might say, a respectable woman who would go to bed with anyone for two hundred louis, or accept a lover on receipt of five hundred a month. Until her twenty-sixth year she continued to make brilliant conquests, ruining three ambassadors, four financiers, two bishops, and three Chevaliers of the Ordres du Roi;

and, as the criminal rarely stops at his first crime – especially when it has been successful – the vicious and guilty Juliette blackened herself with two more of a similar nature. The first was committed in order that she might rob one of her lovers who had entrusted her with a considerable sum of money of which his family knew absolutely nothing; the second, in order that she might more speedily come by a legacy of a hundred thousand francs, which another of her adoring lovers had included in his will in the name of a third person, who was instructed to hand it over to the said lady after his friend's decease.

To these horrors Madame de Lorsange added two or three infanticides. The fear of spoiling her attractive figure, strengthened by the necessity of hiding a double intrigue, several times encouraged her to have abortions; and these crimes, as undiscovered as the others, in no way hindered this clever and ambitious creature from daily finding new dupes and increasing, moment by moment, both her fortune and her crimes. It will thus be seen that it is, unfortunately, only too true that prosperity often accompanies crime, and that from the very bosom of the most deliberate corruption and debauchery men may gild the thread of life with that which they call happiness.

But, in order that this cruel and fatal truth should not alarm the reader, and in order that the sensibilities of honourable and righteous people may not be disturbed by our subsequent example of misfortune and misery relentlessly pursuing virtue, let us immediately state that this prosperity of crime is only apparent, not real. Independently of the punishment certainly reserved by Providence for those who have succeeded in this way, they also nourish in the depths of their hearts a worm which ceaselessly gnaws at them, and prevents them from enjoying the false glow of happiness which they would seize, leaving in its place only the rending memory of those crimes by which they attained it. With regard to the torment of virtue by misfortune, the unfortunate victim whom fate persecutes in this way has his conscience for consolation, and this, together with the secret joy he draws from his purity, soon compensates him for the injustice of men.

Such, then, was the state of the affairs of Madame de Lorsange when M. de Corville, a gentleman of fifty, and enjoying the position in society already described above, resolved to sacrifice himself entirely for this woman, attaching her life permanently with his own. Whether by his attention, his conduct, or the wisdom of Madame de Lorsange, he succeeded, and had been living with her for four years, entirely as with a legitimate wife, when they decided to spend several months during the summer on a superb estate he had lately purchased near Montargis. One evening in June, when the beauty of the weather had tempted them to wander as far as the town, they felt too tired to make their return on foot. Instead, they entered the inn where the Lyons coach makes a stop, intending to send a rider to the château to demand a carriage for their return. They were resting in a low, cool room opening on to the courtyard, when the aforesaid coach drew up before the inn. As it is natural enough to study the comings and goings of travellers – and there is no one who has not whiled away an idle moment with this form of entertainment when it has presented itself – Madame de Lorsange, followed by her lover, arose to watch the coachload of people enter the inn. The vehicle seemed to be empty, until one of the guards, in descending, received in his arms from one of his companions a young girl of about twenty-six or twenty-seven years of age, wrapped in a miserable little calico cloak and bound like a criminal. A cry of horror and surprise escaped from Madame de Lorsange, at which the young girl, turning, revealed such a sweet and delicate countenance, such a slim and graceful figure, that M. de Corville and his mistress could not help being interested in the unfortunate creature. M. de Corville approached the guards and asked one of them what the unfortunate girl had done.

'To tell the truth, monsieur, she has been accused of three or four very serious crimes: robbery, murder and arson. But I must admit that both my companion and myself have never before felt such repugnance over the transport of a criminal – she is the most gentle creature, and seems to us unusually honest . . . '

'Ah!' exclaimed M. de Corville, 'it seems to me that we have here another of those everyday blunders of the lower courts. And where,' he continued, 'was the offence committed?'

'At a hostelry three leagues from Lyons. She was tried at Lyons and is being taken to Paris for confirmation of the sentence. She will, however, be taken back to Lyons for execution.'

Madame de Lorsange, who had drawn close and listened to this recital, whispered quietly to M. de Corville that she wished to hear the story of her misfortunes from the girl's own lips. And M. de Corville, urged by the same desire, made himself known to the guards and asked if this would be possible.

As they were not at all opposed to the idea, it was decided that they should spend the night at Montargis, and two comfortable suites were placed at the disposal of the prisoner and her guardians. The nobleman accepting responsibility for her safety, she was untied and conducted to the apartments of the Comtesse. The guards retired to bed after an early supper; and when the unfortunate girl had been persuaded to take a little nourishment, Madame de Lorsange, unable to restrain the most intense interest, doubtless said to herself: 'This wretched and probably innocent creature is treated as a criminal. On the other hand everything prospers around me – who, assuredly, am much more a criminal than she is!'

Madame de Lorsange, I say, as soon as she saw her young guest a little more at ease, a little consoled by the caresses and attentions lavished on her and the interest taken in her, induced her to describe in some detail the events which had brought such an honest and sensible looking creature into such disastrous circumstances.

'To tell you the story of my life, Madame,' said the beautiful unfortunate, addressing the Comtesse, 'is to offer you the most striking example of the misfortunes of innocence. It would be to accuse providence to complain of it – it would be a sort of crime, and I dare not do it . . .'

Tears flowed abundantly from the eyes of the poor girl. But, having given way to her emotions for a few moments, she regained control of herself and commenced her narrative in these terms.

❧ Four ❧

You will permit me to conceal my name and birth, Madame; without being illustrious it is honourable, nor was I originally destined to the humiliation to which you now see me reduced. I lost my parents while quite young, and thought that, with the little money they left me, I could wait for satisfactory employment. I refused many offers of work because of their dubious nature. And so, without perceiving it, I exhausted my small capital in Paris – where I was born. The poorer I became, the more I found myself despised; the greater my need of assistance, the less did I expect to obtain any. But of all the trials I experienced during the early days of my unhappy situation, of all the horrible proposals made to me, I shall only tell you of the events which befell me at the home of Monsieur Dubourg, one of the wealthiest landlords in the capital. I was sent to him by the woman who kept the boarding-house where I was lodging, and she recommended him as a gentleman whose good name and riches could the most surely alleviate the rigours of my condition. After waiting a very long time in the ante-room of Monsieur Dubourg, I was at last introduced to him. This odd-looking creature, about forty-eight years old, had just got out of bed. He was wrapped in a loose dressing-gown which scarcely hid his disorder; and, when I entered, his servants were dressing his hair. He dismissed them immediately and asked me what I wished for.

'Alas! sir,' I replied, very much confused, 'I am a poor orphan, and despite the fact that I'm not yet fourteen years of age, I am already acquainted with every shade of adversity. I come to beg your pity, to implore your compassion . . .'

And so I related to him every detail in the story of my misfortunes, the difficulty I had experienced in finding work, and the shame I felt about accepting any, especially as I had not been born into such a lowly position. I told him how my money had slowly gone, how I could not find employment, and how I hoped he would be able to offer me a means of livelihood. To be brief, I unburdened myself with all the eloquence dictated by misfortune; an eloquence which rises quickly in a simple and sensitive soul – yet one which is abhorrent to the mind of the opulent . . .

Monsieur Dubourg listened to me, indulging in many distractions the while. He then asked me if I had always been good.

'I should neither be so poor nor so embarrassed, sir,' I replied, 'did I wish to cease being so.'

'But,' exclaimed Monsieur Dubourg, 'by what right do you claim that the wealthy should assist you, while you refuse to be of service to them?'

'Of what service do you pretend to speak, sir?' I enquired, informing him that I desired nothing better than a chance to render those which decency and my age permitted.

He answered me at some length: 'The services of a child like you are but little use for domestic purposes; you are neither old enough nor even strong enough for such as position as you wish. You had far better occupy yourself in pleasing men, and in trying to find some fellow who will consent to take care of you. All this virtue of which you make such a fuss is worthless in the world; you may bow continually at the foot of its altars, yet its vain incense will never feed you. What pleases men least, what they hold in the least esteem, and what they despise above all else, is the so-called wisdom of your sex. Here, in this world, my child, we value only what brings us profit or delight – and of what profit is a woman's virtue to us? Her caprices and her disorders serve us and amuse us, but her chastity never interests us in the slightest. In other words, when men like us grant a request, it is always in the hope of receiving something in return. And how can a little girl like you repay what is done for her, unless she abandons herself completely to us, allowing us all that we may desire of her person?'

'Oh, sir!' I replied, my heart grown heavy with sighs, 'have honesty and benevolence altogether disappeared from the intentions of men?'

'Very nearly,' replied Dubourg; 'people talk about them a great deal, yet why would you have things so? Don't you realise that people have recovered from the mania of obliging *gratis*? – they have discovered that the pleasures of chastity are but the enjoyments of pride; and, as nothing is so rapidly dispersed, have come to prefer more genuine sensations. They realise, for example, that with a child like you, it is infinitely more profitable to reap, as the fruit of their monetary advances, all those pleasures offered by the refinements of lust, rather than the very chilly and unsatisfying ones of handing out alms for nothing. The knowledge of his reputation, enjoyed by a liberal, open-handed, and generous man, never equals in pleasure – even at the instant he enjoys such actions most intensely – the slightest delights of the senses.'

'Oh, sir! When mankind is ruled by principles such as these, there can be nothing left for the unfortunate except to perish!'

'What matter? The population of France is much greater than is necessary; providing its machine always has the same elasticity, what does it matter to the State whether its body is composed of a few more or a few less individuals?'

'But do you believe that children can respect their fathers or their elders when they are ill-treated by them?'

'What does it matter to a father whether the children who trouble him love him or not?'

'It would, then, have been far better had we been smothered in our cradles!'

'Certainly! – Such was once the custom in many countries; amongst the Greeks for instance; and such is the custom of the Chinese: in that country unfortunate children are exposed, or put to death. What is the good of letting such creatures live when they cannot rely on the assistance of their parents – either because these happen to be dead, or because they disclaim their offspring? If such children are allowed to live they only serve to overburden the State by increasing a population which is already too great. Bastards, orphans and deformed children should be condemned to death at birth; the first two classes because they no longer have anyone to watch over them and care for them – and because a childhood endured under such conditions may one day make them dangerous to society; the others because deformed weak-lings can be of no use to society. All children coming within these categories are to society what excrescences become to the flesh: they nourish themselves on the sap of the healthy members, and at the same time weaken them causing them to degenerate. They might be compared with those parasitic plants and vegetables which, attaching themselves to healthy growths, completely spoil these by drawing off their nutritious essence. The funds collected to feed such scum are crying abuses; particularly those richly endowed establishments which are built for such creatures, and at such an expense! As if the human species was so exceedingly rare, so infinitely precious, that it becomes necessary to consider the welfare of its lowest segment! But let us leave the discussion of these policies of which you cannot, my child, comprehend a thing; and as for yourself, why complain of your predicament when the remedy lies within yourself?'

'At what a price, gracious heaven!'

'At the price of a mere chimera, a thing which has no value at all, other than the one which your pride places on it. Briefly,' continued this barbarian, whilst rising and opening the door, 'that is all I can do for you – If you can't agree to my proposition, get out of my sight! I do not like beggars . . .'

My tears flowed; I could not hold them back any longer. Would you believe it, Madame? – they served only to increase the irritable temper of this man, instead of softening him. He slammed the door, and seizing me by the collar of my dress brutally told me that he was going to force me into doing that which I would not willingly grant him. At this cruel moment my misfortune lent me courage; I extricated myself from his arms and threw myself towards the door.

'Loathsome man,' I shouted as I ran; 'may Heaven, so grievously insulted by you, punish you as you deserve for your execrable cruelty and hardness of heart! You are worthy neither of those riches which you put to so vile a use, nor of the air which you breathe in a world stained by your barbarities.'

Reaching my lodgings I hastened to inform my landlady as to the kind of reception given me by the man to whose house she had sent me. But my surprise passed all bounds when I heard this female wretch load me with reproaches instead of sympathetically sharing my grief!

'You mean little creature,' she exclaimed in her rage; 'do you imagine that men are foolish enough to bestow charity on little girls such as yourself without exacting the interest on their money? Monsieur Dubourg is too kind to have acted as he has done. Had I been in his position you would not have escaped from my room before I had satisfied my desires. However, since you do not wish to profit by the help I have offered, I can only let you dispose of yourself as you wish. You owe me rent – by tomorrow you must either pay me my money or go to prison!'

'Madame, have pity on me . . .'

'People starve through indulging in pity.'

'But what would you have me do?'

'You must return to Monsieur Dubourg – you must satisfy him, and bring me back some cash. I shall go and see him and make up, if I can, for your silly behaviour. I shall offer him your apologies. But mind you behave better next time!'

Ashamed and in despair at not knowing which path to take, seeing myself harshly repulsed by everyone, and without any other resource, I told Madame Desroches (that was my landlady's name) that I was ready for everything in order to placate her. She went off to see the financier, and on her return informed me that she had experienced considerable difficulty in prevailing on him to grant me another chance – that only by dint of repeated entreaties had she persuaded him to see me again the following morning. She ended by warning me that I had better keep an eye on my conduct, for if I disappointed him again, or disobeyed him in the least, he would himself undertake the business of having me locked up for life.

Next day I arrived at the mansion quite excited. Dubourg was alone, and in a more indecent state than on the previous evening. Brutality, libertinism, all the marks of debauchery shone forth from his sullen features.

'You have la Desroches to thank for my welcome,' he grumbled in a harsh tone; 'for it is only on her account that I condescend to grant you my kindness for a space. You should certainly feel undeserving of it after your conduct yesterday! Undress immediately! And if you offer anything like the slightest resistance to my desires, two men who are waiting in my ante-room will take you to a place which you will never leave again while there is life in your body . . .'

'Oh, sir!' I wept, throwing myself at the knees of this despicable man, 'relent, allow yourself some mercy, I beseech you! I would rather die a thousand deaths than betray the principles I received during my childhood. Do you not realise that you will no sooner have accomplished your crime than the spectacle of my despair will overwhelm you with remorse . . .'

But the infamies to which Dubourg had abandoned himself whilst I spoke hindered me from proceeding further. I realised the folly of pretending to myself that I could affect a man who found my grief merely a vehicle for the increase of his horrible passions. He became more and more inflamed at my bitter accents, at my weeping and shuddering, relishing them with an inhumanity which frightened me, and further preparing himself for his criminal attempts. He rose to his feet, revealing himself to me in a state in which reason rarely triumphs, and during which the resistance of the object which causes such loss of reason is but an added stimulus to the delirium of the senses. He grasped me brutally; impetuously he tore away those veils which still concealed what he was burning to enjoy; then, in turn, he abused me, flattered me, caressed me, and treated me with contempt . . . Oh! what a picture! Almighty God, what a strange medley of hardness and mad unbridled lust! It seemed as if the Supreme Being, during the first of such circumstances in my life, wished to imprint eternally on my soul an image of all the horror I ought to feel for the kind of crime, or sin, which so often has its genesis in an abundance of evils similar to those with which I was threatened . . . But was there necessity for complaint at this hour? Certainly not – for I owed my very safety to his excesses . . . A little less debauchery and he would have had his will of me; but the fires of Dubourg's ardour were extinguished by the effervescence of his

attempts. Heaven avenged, on my behalf, all the assaults to which the
monster tried to abandon himself – for the loss of his force before the
sacrifice preserved me from becoming his victim.

Nevertheless, Dubourg only became the more insulting. He accused
me of being the cause of his weakness, and wished to recompense
himself by fresh outrages and abuses of an even more terrifying nature.
There was nothing disgusting he did not say to me, nothing he did not
attempt, nothing his vile imagination, the hardness of his nature, and
his depraved morals did not cause him to undertake. But my awkward-
ness tired his patience, especially as I made not the slightest attempt to
play up to him. You may well imagine that it required considerable
fortitude on my part to lend myself in such a manner; nor has the
passage of time been able to obliterate my remorse . . . Nothing,
however, succeeded; his final attempts failed miserably; and my submission lost its power to inflame him. In vain he successively passed
from tenderness to severity, from severity to tyranny, from glances of
loving sympathy to the excesses of filth and lust. At length we were
equally tired – a condition which fortunately persisted and prevented
his being able to recover the ability necessary for truly dangerous
attacks. He gave over, but made me promise to return the following
day; and in order to be absolutely sure of this he paid me only the sum I
owed la Desroches. And so I returned to the woman's house exceedingly humbled by my adventure, and firmly decided, whatever might
happen to me in the future, never to expose myself to this man a third
time. I expressed these ideas to my landlady when paying her, and
decried with maledictions the old rogue who had been capable of so
cruelly taking advantage of my misery. Nevertheless, my curses, far
from bringing on him the wrath of God, seemed only to bring him
good fortune. Eight days later I learned that this notorious libertine
had just received from the government a grant which increased his
annual revenue to more than 400,000 livres. I was lost in reflections on
this and similar inconsistencies of destiny, when a ray of hope seemed
suddenly to lighten my heart.

La Desroches came to tell me that at last she had discovered a house
where I would gladly be received, providing I conducted myself well
therein.

'Oh! Merciful Heaven,' I cried delightedly, flinging myself into her
arms, ' – that is the very condition I should myself lay down; do not
doubt my decision for an instant – I accept the offer with pleasure . . . '

And so I left the home of Desroches for what I hoped would be a
changed and better period of life.

My new master was an old usurer who had become rich not only by way of lending money, but also by robbing everyone with whom he came into contact – whenever he found it possible to do so safely and with impunity. He lived on the rue Quincampoix, in an apartment on the first floor, accompanied by an old mistress whom he called his wife and who was at least as wicked as he himself.

'Sophie,' said this miser to me (for that was the name I had assumed in order to conceal my own), 'my dear Sophie, the first of the virtues necessary to anyone who lives in my house is that of honesty . . . And if ever I should find you appropriating to yourself the tenth part of one of my pennies, I shall have you hanged – hanged, do you understand, until it would be impossible to revive you! For if my wife and I are able to enjoy a few small pleasures in our old age, it is only because it is the fruit of our excessive labours and profound sobriety. By the way, my child, do you eat a lot?'

'Only a few ounces of bread a day, sir,' I replied; 'together with a little water and some soup when I am lucky enough to be able to have it.'

'Soup! Soup! – good heavens!' exclaimed the old miser to his wife – 'Let us bewail the extravagance of luxury and its progress in our times!' Then he continued: 'For a year this child has been looking for a job; for a year she has been dying of starvation; and at the same time she wants to eat soup! We ourselves have it only rarely – once every Sunday, to be precise – we who have worked ourselves like galley-slaves for forty years. You will receive three ounces of bread a day, my girl, half a bottle of river water, and every eighteen months one of my wife's old dresses from which you can make your petticoats. At the end of a year, if we are satisfied with your services, and if your approach to economy corresponds with our own; if, in short, you order arrangements so that our domestic matters prosper, then we will pay you three crowns.

'Looking after us is only a small matter. It is simply a case of cleaning and polishing this six-roomed flat three times each week. And, of course, you will make the beds, answer the door, powder my wig, dress the hair of my wife, look after the dog, the cat, and the parrot, attend to your kitchen duties, and wash the dishes regularly, whether they have been used or not; as well as helping my wife with the cooking and spending your spare time making caps, knitting stockings, and producing other little things for the household. So you see, Sophie, there isn't much to do, and you will have quite enough leisure in which to attend to your own odd jobs and make whatever clothing you may need.'

You can easily imagine, Madame, that one would have to be in precisely that state of misery in which I happened to be before you would have accepted such a position. Not only were these creatures asking me to do far more work than my age and strength permitted, but was it possible to keep going on the food and the pittance they offered? Nevertheless I was careful not to be difficult, and installed myself in their home that same evening.

If, Madame, the cruel situation in which I found myself allowed me to think of amusing you for a moment – when I ought only to try and arouse sympathetic feeling for me in your heart – I honestly believe I could send you into paroxysms of laughter by relating in detail some of the manifestations of avarice which abounded so plentifully in that house. But such a terrible catastrophe befell me during my second year there that, when I think of it, I find it difficult to offer humorous details before acquainting you with the nature of this misfortune. Nevertheless, I can tell you, Madame, that lights were never used in that house. The bedroom of my master and mistress was situated directly opposite the street lamp, so they dispensed with any other means of illumination, not even using a light to see their way to bed. As for underwear and suchlike, they never wore it, but sewed into the sleeves of their coats and dresses old ruffles, which I washed each Saturday evening, so that they would be clean and fresh for Sunday. Neither were there any sheets or towels, so as to avoid the expense of laundering – for this, according to the respectable Monsieur du Harpin, was an unusually expensive item. They never had wine in the house, for, according to Madame du Harpin, clear water was the natural beverage of the first men, and the only one prescribed us by nature. Every time bread was cut a basket had to be placed underneath the loaf so as to catch the crumbs. To these were added the remnants of every meal, and on Sundays the mixture was fried in a little rancid butter and served up to form the special dish of the Sabbath day. Clothes and upholstery were never brushed in the usual manner, as that might have tended to produce wear in the material. Instead they were lightly swept with a feather duster. Their shoes were reinforced with metal caps, and each of them kept, as venerable relics, those which they had worn on their wedding day. But a much more bizarre duty was one which I had to undertake once a week. There was one large room in the flat with completely bare walls. Here I used to go regularly in order to scrape some of the plaster off the walls with a knife. This was then passed through a fine sieve, and I was instructed to use the resulting powder each morning to dress the gentleman's wig and the chignon of the lady.

I would to God that these were the only depraved methods of economy indulged by this sorry couple. Nothing is more natural than the desire to conserve one's means; but what is not equally so is the wish to increase them with the fortunes of others – and it did not take me long to realise that it was in this manner that Monsieur Du Harpin had become so rich.

Now at that time there was living above us an individual in very easy circumstances, owning some very pretty jewels; and these, perhaps because they belonged to our neighbour, or perhaps because they had actually passed through his hands, were well known to my master. Quite frequently I heard him lamenting to his wife about a certain gold box worth thirty or forty louis, which, he said, would certainly have belonged to him if he had been a little more adroit at an earlier time. In order to console himself for having returned the box which he had once borrowed, Monsieur Du Harpin planned to steal it, and it was me he commanded to effect this transference.

Having delivered a long speech on the unimportance of stealing, and on the possible utility to society of such an activity – since it served to re-establish an equilibrium totally upset by the unequal distribution of wealth, Monsieur Du Harpin presented me with a false key, assuring me that it would open the apartment of our neighbour, and that I would find the box in a desk which was never locked. He added that I would be able to remove it without any danger, and that for such a considerable service he would add an extra crown to my wages for the following two years.

'Oh, Monsieur!' I cried, 'is it possible that a master dares attempt to corrupt his servant in such a manner? What is to prevent me from turning against you the very weapons which you have placed in my hands? And how could you reasonably object if I robbed you according to your own principles?'

Monsieur Du Harpin, astonished at my reply, did not dare insist further. He reacted by nursing a secret grudge against me; but explained his behaviour by pretending he had been testing me, saying that it was fortunate I had not succumbed to his insidious suggestions as otherwise I should have been hanged. I accepted his explanation, but from that time onwards I felt both the misfortunes with which such a proposition menaced me, and how unwise I had been to answer so firmly. Nevertheless, there had been no middle way; for I had been faced with the choice of actually committing the crime, or of obstinately rejecting the proposal. Had I been a little more experienced I should have left the house at that instant; but it had already been written on the page of my destiny that every honest impulse in my character would have to be paid for by some misfortune. I was therefore obliged to submit to circumstances without any possibility of escape.

Monsieur Du Harpin allowed almost a month to pass – that is to say nearly the turn of my second year in his employ – and never said a word, or showed the least resentment at my refusal. Then one evening, my work being finished and having just retired to my room for a few hours of rest, I suddenly heard the door thrown open, and saw, not without fear, Monsieur Du Harpin accompanied by a police official and four soldiers of the watch who immediately surrounded my bed.

'Perform your duties, officer,' he said to the police official. 'This miserable creature has stolen a diamond of mine worth a thousand crowns. You will almost certainly find it in her room, or on her person!'

'But, sir! You cannot possibly think I have robbed you,' I cried, throwing myself, in consternation, at the foot of my bed. 'Ah! who knows better than you how repugnant such an action would be to me, and how impossible it is that I should commit it!'

But Monsieur Du Harpin made a great commotion so that nobody could hear what I was saying, and so contrived to order the search that the miserable ring was found in my mattress. In face of such proof there could be no reply. Therefore I was immediately seized, hand-cuffed, and ignominiously led to the Prison du Palais – without a word being heard of the many things I could have said in my defence.

The trial of those unfortunate wretches who lack both influence and protection is quickly over in France. For it is believed that virtue is incompatible with poverty; and misfortune, in our courts, is accepted as conclusive proof against the accused. An unjust bias causes a presumption that the person who might possibly have committed the crime actually did commit it. The feelings of one's judges thus take their measure from the situation in which one is found – and if titles or wealth are not available to prove the honesty of the accused, the impossibility of his being so is immediately accepted as demonstrated.

Well might I defend myself; well might I furnish an exact description of the true state of affairs to the state lawyer who was sent to question me. My master accused me in court – the diamond had been found in my room; therefore, clearly, I must have stolen it. When I wished to describe Monsieur Du Harpin's horrible deed, and to show how the misfortune which had befallen me was simply a consequence of his vengeance, of his obsessive desire to ruin a creature who knowing his secrets was in a position to wield considerable power over him, they interpreted my complaints as recriminations, and informed me that Monsieur Du Harpin had been known for forty years as a man of integrity and was quite incapable of such an outrage. Thus it was that I found myself about to pay with my life for my refusal to participate in a criminal conspiracy – when an unexpected happening set me free, once more to plunge me into the further miseries still awaiting me in the world outside.

A woman of forty named Dubois, celebrated for her indulgence in every species or horror, was likewise on the eve of her execution – which at least was more deserved than mine, since her crimes had been established while mine did not exist.

Somehow or other I had inspired a kind of sympathy in this woman and one evening, a few days before each of us was due to lose her life, she told me not to go to bed, but to remain as unobtrusively close to her as I could.

'Between midnight and one o'clock in the morning,' explained this prosperous villain, 'the prison will be set on fire . . . thanks to my machinations. Someone may be burned, but what does that matter? The certain thing is that we shall make our escape. Three men, accomplices and friends of mine, will meet us, and I can answer to you for your liberty.'

The hand of heaven, which had just punished my innocence, became the servant of crime so far as my protectress was concerned. Once the fire had started the conflagration became terrible. Ten people were burned alive, but we made our escape in safety. The same day we managed to reach the cottage of a poacher who lived in the forest of Bondy. He was thus a different kind of rogue, yet nevertheless an intimate friend of our band.

'Now you are free, my dear Sophie,' la Dubois said to me, 'and you can choose whatever kind of life seems to suit you best; but if you listen to me you will renounce your virtuous ways, which, as you see, have never succeeded in helping you. Your misplaced delicacy conducted you right to the foot of the gallows, yet a frightful crime has saved me from a similar fate. Just look at the value which goodness has in the world, and then consider whether it is worth dying for. You are young and pretty; and, if you like, I will take care of your future in Brussels. I am going there, because that is where I was born, and within two years I can place you at the very peak of fortune. But I warn you that it will certainly not be by the narrow paths of virtue that I will promote your success. At your age it is necessary to engage in more than one profession, as well as to serve in more than one intrigue, if you wish to make your way to the top with any promptitude. Do you understand me, Sophie? – Do you understand me? Decide quickly because we must be on the move. We are safe here only for a few hours.'

'Oh, Madame,' I replied to my benefactress, 'I am obliged to you for so much, since you have saved my life; yet it fills me with despair when I consider that this was possible only by way of the commission of a crime. And you may be very sure that had it been necessary for me to participate in it I would rather have died than done so. I know but too well the dangers I have courted in abandoning myself to those sentiments of honesty which for ever spring up in my heart, but whatever the thorns of virtue may be I shall always prefer them to the false glow of prosperity and those unreliable advantages which momentarily accompany crime. Thanks be to heaven, my religious convictions will never desert me, and if providence renders my way of life difficult it is only in order the more abundantly to recompense me in a better world. It is this hope which consoles me, this hope which softens all my griefs, calms my complaints, fortifies me in adversity and enables me fearlessly to encounter any evils with which I may be faced. This joy would immediately be extinguished in my heart were I to stain myself with crime – and, to the fear of even more terrible reverses in this world, I should add the frightening expectation of those punishments which celestial justice reserves in the beyond for those who outrage it.'

'I'm afraid you have some absurd ideas which will quickly take you to the workhouse, my girl,' exclaimed la Dubois, frowning. 'Believe me, you will be well advised to give up your ideas of celestial justice, of punishment, or rewards to come. Those things are all best forgotten as soon as you leave school, for their only result is to help cause you to starve to death – if you are stupid enough to believe them once you have launched out on a life of your own. The hardness of the rich justifies the rascality of the poor, my child; if humanity reigned in their hearts, then virtue would become established in ours; but so long as our misfortunes, and our patience in enduring them, so long as our good faith and our submission serve only to multiply our chains, then we can lay our crimes at their door, and we would be fools indeed were we to refuse to profit by them when they can to some extent ameliorate the yoke with which we are burdened.

'Nature caused us all to be born equal, Sophie; and if chance has been pleased to disorganise the original plan of her general laws, it is for us to correct such caprices, and to recover, by our adroitness, the usurpations of those who are stronger than us. I love to hear them – those rich gentlemen, those judges and magistrates – I love to hear them preach of virtue to us. It must be very difficult to avoid theft when one has three times more than is necessary for living in comfort; it must be equally difficult never to think of murder when one is surrounded only by the adulations of sycophants, or the submission of absolute slaves; likewise it must be enormously distressing to be temperate and sober when one is perpetually surrounded by the most succulent delicacies; and people must experience a great deal of trouble in being honest when they have no reason to lie.

'But we, Sophie, we whom this barbarous providence which you are foolish enough to idolise has condemned to crawl on the earth as a serpent crawls in the grass – we who are disdained because we are poor, humiliated because we are weak, and who at length find nothing but bitterness and care over the whole surface of the globe – could you wish us to forbear from crime when it is her hand alone which opens for us the door of life, sustains and maintains life in us, and saves us from losing it? You would, it seems, prefer us to be perpetually submissive and humble whilst those who control us retain for themselves every favour which fortune can grant, we having only the experience of pain, hardship, and sorrow, with the addition of tears, the iron-mark of infamy, and, finally, the scaffold!

'No, Sophie, no – either this providence which you so revere has been created solely for our scorn – or that is not the intention. . . . Get to know it better, get to know it better and you will soon be convinced that whenever it places us in a position where evil becomes necessary for us, granting us at the same time the possibility of exercising this evil, it is because evil, just as much as good, serves its laws; and it gains equally as much from the one as from the other. We were created in a state of equality, and the man who disturbs this state is not more culpable than he who seeks to re-establish it. Both men are activated by given motives, and each must follow his impulse, tying a bandage round his eyes and enjoying the game.'

I confess that if ever I was shaken it was by the seductions of this clever woman. But a voice louder than hers combatted the sophisms she wished to plant in my heart. I listened to it, and asserted for the last time that I had decided never to allow myself to be corrupted.

'Ah, well!' exclaimed Dubois. 'Do what you wish. I leave you to your evil fate – but if ever you happen to get yourself hanged, which you can hardly escape since the destiny which watches over crime inevitably sacrifices virtue, remember, at least, never to mention us.'

While we were reasoning in this fashion, the three companions of la Dubois were drinking with the poacher; and, as wine commonly has the effect of causing the malefactor to forget his past criminal offences, often inviting him to augment them at the very edge of the precipice from which he has just escaped, so did the miscreant wretches who surrounded me feel a desire to amuse themselves at my expense before I had time to run away from them. Their principles, their morals, combined with the sinister location in which we found ourselves, and the apparent security from the law which they felt they at present enjoyed, together with their drunkenness, my age, my innocence, and my figure, all encouraged them in their project. They rose from the table, held counsel amongst themselves and consulted la Dubois – proceedings the mystery of which made me shudder with horror, and which resulted in my having to decide whether, before leaving them, I would pass through the hands of all four willingly or by force. If I did it willingly they would each give me a crown to help me on my way, since I had refused to accompany them. If, on the other hand, they were obliged to use force to settle the matter, the thing would be done all the same, but the last of the four to enjoy me would plunge a knife into my breast and they would bury me immediately afterwards at the foot of a tree.

I leave you to imagine, Madame, the effect which this execrable proposition had on me. I threw myself at the feet of la Dubois, begging her to be my protectress yet a second time; but the villainous creature just laughed at my terrifying situation – which to her seemed a mere nothing.

'Gracious heavens!' she said, ' – just look at you, so miserable and unhappy simply because you are obliged to serve successively four big boys built like these! In Paris, my girl, there must be ten thousand women who would hand over plenty of beautiful crowns if they could be in the position you are in at the moment . . . Listen,' she added, after thinking things over for a few seconds, 'I have enough control over these sly fellows to obtain mercy for you, if you wish to prove yourself worthy of it.'

'What must I do, Madame,' I cried in tears. 'Instruct me! – I am quite ready to carry out your orders . . . '

'Follow us, become one of our band, and do the same things as we do without the slightest repugnance. For this price I can guarantee you the rest . . . '

Consideration did not seem necessary to me. I agree that in accepting I ran the risk of new dangers; but these were less pressing than those immediately facing me. I would be able to avoid them; whilst nothing could help me escape those with which I was menaced.

'I will go wherever you wish, Madame,' I said; 'I promise you I will go anywhere – only save me from the lusts of these men and I will never leave you!'

'Boys,' said la Dubois to the four bandits, 'this girl is now a member of our gang. I accept her and I approve her. I forbid you, moreover, to do her any violence. And you mustn't disgust her with our business on her first day. Just consider how useful her age and face can be to us, and let's use them to our interest instead of sacrificing her to our pleasures . . . '

But once roused, the passions can reach such a pitch in a man that no voice is able to recall them into captivity; and those with whom I was dealing were in no state to hear anything at all. All four of them, in fact, immediately surrounded me, and in a condition least calculated to enable me to expect mercy, declaring unanimously to la Dubois that since I was in their hands there *was* no reason why I should not become their prey.

'First me!' said one of them, seizing me round the waist.

'And by what right do you claim the first turn?' exclaimed a second, pushing his comrade aside and tearing me brutally from his arms.

'You shan't have her until I've finished!' shouted a third.

And the dispute becoming heated, our four champions tore each other's hair, flung each other on the ground, sent each other flying head over heels and rained blows on one another. As for me I was only too happy to see them all involved in a situation which gave me the chance to escape. So while la Dubois was occupied in trying to separate them I quickly ran away, soon reaching the forest. In a moment the house had disappeared from view.

'Oh, Being Most Supreme,' I exclaimed, throwing myself to my knees as soon as I felt myself secure from pursuit, ' – Being Supreme, my only true protector and my guide, deign to take pity on my misery. You know my weakness and my innocence. You know with what confidence I place in you my every hope. Deign to snatch me from the dangers which pursue me; or by a death less shameful than that which I have recently escaped, recall me promptly to your eternal peace.'

Prayer is the sweetest consolation of the unfortunate. One is stronger after prayer. And so I rose full of courage. But, as it was growing dark, I wound my way deep into a copse so as to pass the night with less risk. The safety in which I believed myself, my exhaustion, and the little joy I was tasting, all contributed to help me pass a good night. The sun was already high when I opened my eyes to its light. The moment of awakening is, however, calamitous for the unhappy; for, after the rest of the bodily senses, the cessation of thought, and the instantaneous forgetfulness of sleep, the memory of misfortune seems to leap into the mind with a newness of life which makes its weight all the more onerous to bear.

'Ah, well,' I said to myself, 'it seems to be true that there are some human beings whom nature destines to live under the same conditions as wild beasts. Living hidden in their retreats, flying from men like the animals, what difference remains between man and beast? Is it worth while being born to endure so pitiful a fate?'

And my tears flowed abundantly as these sad reflections formed themselves in my mind. Barely had I ceased thinking after this manner when I heard a noise somewhere near me. For a moment I thought it was some creatures of the wood; then, little by little, I distinguished the voices of two men.

'Come along, my friend, come along,' said one of them, 'We shall do wonderfully well here. And my mother's cruel and deadly presence shall no longer prevent me from tasting with you, at least for a few moments, those pleasures which are so dear to me.'

They drew nearer, placing themselves so directly in front of me that not a word they spoke, not a movement they made, could escape me. And then I saw –

'In heaven's name, Madame,' said Sophie, interrupting her narrative, 'is it possible that fate has never placed me in any situations but those so critical that it becomes as difficult for modesty to hear them as to depict them? . . . That horrible crime which outrages both nature and law, that frightful offence upon which the hand of God has fallen heavily so many times, that infamy, in a word, so new to me that I only understood it with difficulty – this I saw, consummated before my very eyes, with all the impure excitations, all the frightful episodes which it is possible for premeditated depravity to conjure up.'

One of the men – he who assumed the dominating role – was about twenty-four years old. He was wearing a green coat, and well enough dressed to cause me to think that he came of good family. The other was probably a young domestic of his house, around seventeen or eighteen and with a very pretty face and figure. The scene which followed was as lengthy as it was scandalous; and the passage of time seemed even more cruel to me, for I dared not move for fear of being discovered.

At last the criminal actors who had played this scene before me, satiated, no doubt, arose to make their way to the road which must have led to their home. But the master, coming near the thicket where I was hiding so that he might relieve himself, my high bonnet betrayed me.

He saw it immediately: 'Jasmin,' he called to his young Adonis, 'we have been discovered, my dear . . . A girl, a profane creature has seen our mysteries! Come, let's get this hussy out of here and find out what she's been doing.'

I did not give them the trouble of helping me out of my hiding place, but quickly jumped up and threw myself at their feet.

'Good gentlemen,' I cried, extending my arms towards them, 'kindly take pity on an unfortunate creature whose fate is more to be commiserated than you might think. Few of the reverses which men meet in life can be equal to mine. Do not let the situation in which you have found me arouse your suspicions, for it is the result of my poverty rather than my errors. Instead of increasing the sum of evils which crush me, you can, on the contrary, diminish it by helping me find a means of escape from the misfortunes which continually pursue me.

Monsieur de Bressac, for that was the name of the young man into whose hands I had fallen, had an undue amount of the libertine in his character, but had not been provided with an equal abundance of compassion in his heart. It is, nevertheless, unfortunately only too common to see the debauchery of the senses completely extinguish pity in man. In fact the usual effect of such a life seems to be that of hardening the heart. Whether the greater number of such deviations arise on the basis of a kind of apathy in the soul, or whether they are the result of the violent shock which they imprint on the mass of nerves – thus diminishing the sensitive action of these – it can always be said that a professional debauchee is rarely a man of pity. But, to this natural cruelty in the kind of person whose character I have sketched, there was in Monsieur de Bressac such a marked and additional disgust for our sex, such an inveterate hatred for all that distinguishes it, that it was extremely difficult for me to encourage in his soul those sentiments by which I longed to see him moved.

'Anyway, my little wood-pigeon, just what are you doing here?'

Such was the only response of this man whom I wished to soften, and it was spoken harshly enough.

'Tell me the truth! – You saw everything that happened between this young man and myself, didn't you?'

'Me? – Oh no, Monsieur!' I cried quickly, believing I did no wrong in disguising the truth. 'You may rest assured that I saw only the most ordinary things. I saw you, your friend and yourself, seated together on the grass. I believe I noticed that you chatted together for a moment. But rest completely assured that is all I saw!'

'I would like to believe you,' replied Monsieur de Bressac, 'if only for your own safety. For if I suspected for an instant that you had seen anything else you would certainly never leave this thicket. Come, Jasmin, it is early enough, and we have time to listen to this slut's adventures. She shall recount them to us immediately; and then we can tie her to this great oak and try out our hunting knives on her body.

The young men sat down and ordered me to sit near them. Then I told them, quite truthfully, all that had happened to me since I had found myself alone in the world.

'Jasmin,' said Monsieur de Bressac, rising as soon as I had finished, 'let us be just for once in our lives, my dear. The equitable Themis has already condemned this hussy, and we cannot allow the goddess's wishes to be so cruelly frustrated. We shall ourselves execute upon this criminal the sentence she has incurred. What we are about to commit is not a crime, my friend, it is a virtue, a re-establishment of the order of things. And as we sometimes have the misfortune to disorganise this order, let us courageously right matters – at least when the opportunity presents itself.'

And the heartless men, having pulled me from my place, dragged me towards the tree they had spoken of, without being touched either by my sobs or my tears.

'Tie her here, in this manner,' said Bressac to his valet, as he held me with my belly against the tree.

Using their garters and their handkerchiefs, in a moment they had me so painfully tied down that it was impossible for me to move a single muscle. This operation achieved, the villains removed my skirts, lifted my chemise as high as my shoulders, and took out their hunting knives. I thought for a minute that they were going to cleave open my posteriors which had been uncovered by their brutality.

'That's enough,' said Bressac before I had received a single cut. 'That's enough to acquaint her with what we could do to her, to keep her dependent on us. Sophie,' he continued, as he untied the cords, 'dress yourself, be discreet, and follow us. If you remain loyal to me, my child, you shall have no excuse for repentance. My mother needs a second chambermaid, and I am going to present you to her. On the strength of your story I can guarantee your conduct to her; but if you abuse my kindness or betray my confidence – then remember this tree which will become your death bed. It is only a mile or two from the castle to which we are taking you, and at the slightest fault you will be brought back here.'

Already dressed, I could scarcely find words to thank my benefactor. I threw myself at his feet, embraced his knees, and gave him every assurance possible as to my good behaviour. But he was as insensible to my joy as he had been to my suffering.

'Let's get going,' he exclaimed. 'Your conduct will speak for you, and that alone will decide your fate.'

We continued to make our way. Jasmin and his master talked together, and I followed them humbly without saying word. In less than an hour we arrived at the castle of Madame la Comtesse de Bressac, and its magnificence gave me the impression that whatever position I should fill in this household it would assuredly be more lucrative than that of housekeeper to Monsieur and Madame Du Harpin. I was made to wait in one of the servants' rooms, where Jasmin gave me a very good lunch. Meanwhile Monsieur de Bressac went up to see his mother, told her all about me and, half an hour later, came to find me himself so that he might introduce me to her.

Madame de Bressac was a woman of forty-five, still very beautiful; and she appeared to be extremely honourable and courteous – but, above all, very kind and human. Nevertheless, a little severity seemed blended in her manner and her speech. She had lost her husband two years previously. He had been a man of unusually distinguished family, but had married her with no other fortune than the celebrated name he gave her. Thus all the benefits which the young Marquis de Bressac could hope for depended on his mother, since what his father had been able to leave him was scarcely enough to live on. Madame de Bressac, however, had augmented this by a considerable allowance. But much more would have been necessary to meet the enormous, as well as the irregular, expenses of her son. There were at least sixty thousand livres of revenue in this house and Monsieur de Bressac had neither brothers nor sisters. Nobody had been able to persuade him to enter the army – for everything which separated him from his chosen pleasures was so insupportable to him that it was impossible to make him accept any tie. For three months of the year the Comtesse and her son lived on their country estate, the remainder of their time being spent in Paris. And these three months, which she insisted her son spend with her, were already a severe torture for a man who could never leave the centre of his pleasures without giving way to despair.

The Marquis de Bressac ordered me to tell his mother the same things which I had related to him; and when I had finished my recital she looked at me and said: 'Your candour and your naïvety do not permit me to doubt your innocence. I shall ask no further questions of you, except that I would like to know if you are really, as you say, the daughter of the gentleman you have mentioned. If such is the case, I knew your father, and it will give me yet another reason for being even more interested in your welfare. As for your affair at the Du Harpin household, I shall take it upon myself to bring that to a satisfactory conclusion with a couple of visits to the Chancellor – who has been my friend for many years. He is the greatest man of integrity in France, and it will only be necessary to prove your innocence to him in order to bring to naught everything that has been done against you. Then you will be able to reappear in Paris without the slightest fear . . . But reflect well, Sophie – everything I promise you here is only to be given at the price of the most perfect behaviour. In this way whatever I ask of you will always turn to your profit.'

I threw myself at the feet of Madame de Bressac, assuring her that she would never be anything other than pleased with me; and from that moment I was installed in her home in the position of second chambermaid. After three days the enquiries which Madame de

Bressac had made in Paris concerning me brought in all the confirmation I could desire. Every idea of misfortune evaporated at last from my mind, never to be replaced save by the hope of the sweetest consolations I could possibly expect. But it was not written in heaven that poor Sophie should ever be happy, and if a few moments of calm were fortuitously granted her, it was only to render more bitter those horrors which were to follow.

We had barely arrived in Paris before Madame de Bressac began to work for my benefit. A high official asked to see me, listening to my misfortunes with interest. The dishonesty of Du Harpin was thoroughly investigated and fully admitted, and my questioners were convinced that even if I had profited by the fire in the court prisons, at least I had had nothing to do with the starting of it. Finally all proceedings against me were erased from the records (a matter on which they assured me), and the examining magistrates no longer found it necessary to engage in further formalities.

It is easy to imagine the extent to which such circumstances attached me to Madame de Bressac – even had she not shown me many additional kindnesses. Considering such acts as these, how could I be anything other than bound for ever to such a precious protectress? It had, nevertheless, been far from the intentions of the young Marquis de Bressac that I should become so intimately devoted to his mother. Quite apart from the frightful dissipations in which the young man wallowed, the nature of which I have already revealed to you, and into which he plunged with an even more blind prodigality than he had in the country, I was not long in noticing that he absolutely detested the Comtesse. It is true that she did everything in the world to prevent his debauches – or to interfere with them. But she employed, perhaps, too much severity and the Marquis, inflamed even more by the effects of this stringency, gave himself up to libertinism with even greater ardour. Thus the poor Comtesse drew no profit from her persecutions other than that of making herself the object of a sovereign hate.

'You mustn't imagine,' the Marquis often said to me, 'that my mother acts in your interest entirely of her own volition. Believe me, Sophie, if I didn't pester her continually, she would scarcely remember the promises she made you. You value her every act, yet all she does has been suggested by me. I am not, therefore, claiming too much when I say that it is only to me that you owe any gratitude. What I demand in return should seem to you even more disinterested, since you are well enough acquainted with my tastes to be quite certain that, however pretty you may be, I shall never lay any claim to your favours. No, Sophie, no, the services I expect of you are of quite another kind. And when you are fully convinced of all I have done for you, I hope that I shall find in your heart everything I have a right to expect.'

These speeches seemed so obscure to me that I never knew how to reply to them. I made random remarks, however – and with perhaps a little too much facility.

Which brings me, Madame, to the moment when I must inform you of the only real fault for which I have felt any need to reproach myself during the whole of my life. While I am describing it as a fault, it was certainly an unparalleled extravagance, but at least it was not a crime. It was a simple enough error, and one for which only I myself was punished; but it also seems to me one which heaven's equitable hand ought not to have employed to draw me into the abyss which, unknown to me, was opening beneath my feet. It had been impossible for me to see the Marquis de Bressac without feeling myself attracted to him by an impulse of tenderness which nothing had been able to quell in me. Whatever reflections I may have made on his lack of interest in women, on the depravity of his tastes, on the moral distances which separated us, nothing, nothing in the world could extinguish this nascent passion. And if the Marquis had asked me for my life, I would have sacrificed it to him a thousand times, feeling that such an action would be as nothing. He was far from suspecting the feelings I entertained for him, as these were carefully locked up in my heart . . . Ungrateful as he was, he could never discern the cause of those tears which the miserable Sophie shed, day after day, over the shameful disorders which were destroying him. It was, nevertheless, impossible that he could avoid noticing my personal attention to him; for, blinded by my devotion, I went even so far as to serve his errors – at least in so far as decency permitted me – and I always concealed them from his mother.

My conduct had thus earned me something of his confidence, and each small thing he said to me became precious. I allowed myself, in short, to become so dazzled by the little he offered my heart that there were times when I was arrogant enough to believe that I was not indifferent to him. But time after time the excess of his disorders would promptly disabuse me. They were such that not only was the house filled with servants given up to the same execrable tastes as the Marquis, but he even hired outside a crowd of bad characters whom he visited, or who came to see him day by day. And as such tastes, odious as they are, are not the least expensive, the young man disorganised his finances prodigiously. Sometimes I took the liberty of representing to him all the inconveniences of his conduct. He would listen to me without repugnance, but always ended by explaining that it was impossible to correct the kind of vice by which he was dominated and which reproduced itself under a thousand diverse forms. There was a different nuance of this deviation for every age of man, offering continually new sensations every ten years, and thus enabling it to hold its unfortunate devotees in bondage right to the very edge of the grave . . . But if I attempted to speak to him of his mother and the sorrow he brought her, he would show nothing but vexation, ill-humour, irritation, and impatience. And when he considered for how long she had held a fortune which he felt should already be his, he expressed the most inveterate hatred for this honourable and upright woman, backed by the most unswerving revolt against natural sentiment. Is it then true that when one has so definitely transgressed against the sacred rules of morality and sobriety, the necessary consequence of one's first crime should be a frightful facility in committing all the others with impunity?

Several times I tried to employ religious argument with him. Nearly always being consoled by my own faith, I attempted to transmit some of its sweetness to the soul of this perverse creature, for I was convinced that I might captivate him by these means if only I could tempt him for a moment to partake of their delights. But the Marquis did not long allow me to employ such methods. The declared enemy of our holy mysteries, a self-opinionated and obstinate railer against the purity of our doctrines, a passionate antagonist against the existence of a Supreme Being, Monsieur de Bressac, instead of being converted by me, sought all the more to corrupt me.

'All religions are based on a false principle, Sophie,' he would say to me. 'All accept the cult of a creative being as a necessity. But if this eternal world, like all those others amongst which it floats in the infinite plains of space – if this eternal world has never had a beginning, and will never have an end – if all the products of nature are the results or effects of laws by which she herself is enchained – if her perpetual action and reaction indicate the essential evolution of her being, what becomes of the author whom you so gratuitously lend her?

'Condescend to believe, Sophie, that the God you accept is simply the fruit of ignorance on the one side – and of tyranny on the other. When the strong wished to enslave the weak, they persuaded them that a god had sanctified the chains with which they overwhelmed them; and the oppressed victims, stupefied by their distress, believed everything their masters wished to tell them. All religions are the fatal consequence of this primary fiction and should, together with their origin, be condemned to the utmost scorn. There is not a single one of them but bears the emblems of imposture and stupidity. In all of them I see mysteries which make the reason shudder, dogma which outrages nature, and grotesque ceremonies which cannot but inspire derision. I had scarcely opened my eyes on this world, Sophie, when I learned to detest these horrors. So I decided that I would crush them under my feet, vowing never to return to them throughout my days. If you wish to be sensible you will imitate me.'

'Oh, sir,' I replied, 'you would deprive an unfortunate of her sweetest hope, were you to rob her of the religion which consoles her. Firmly attached to its precepts, absolutely convinced that every blow aimed against it is simply the result of libertinage and the passions, how could I sacrifice to these sophisms – which make me shudder – the sweetest idea in my life?'

To these words I added a thousand other arguments dictated by reason, pouring them forth from my heart. But the Marquis only laughed; and his deceptive principles, nourished by a more masculine eloquence, and supported by studies which, fortunately, I had never been able to indulge, always seemed to upset my arguments. The pious and virtuous Madame de Bressac was not ignorant that her son supported his faults and deviations on all the paradoxes of scepticism, and she often bewailed the fact with me. Then, as she seemed to find me a little more intelligent than the other women who surrounded her, she began to take pleasure in entrusting me with all her sorrows.

Meanwhile her son's evil conduct increased. He had reached the point of not attempting to hide it; and not only had he surrounded his mother with that dangerous and motley crowd submissive to his pleasures, but he had pushed insolence so far as to declare before me that if she took it into her head to thwart his practices he would convince her of their inherent charm by giving himself up to them before her very eyes. I groaned at these proposals and the prospect of such conduct; and in the depths of my being I tried to extract from them a motive for stifling the unfortunate passion which devoured my soul . . . But is love a malady which can easily be cured? Every means by which I sought to oppose it only stirred the flame so that it burned more brightly, and the perfidious Bressac never seemed to me more amiable than when I had ruminated on all those things for which I should have hated him.

During four years I remained in this house, always persecuted by the same woes and always comforted by the same sweetnesses, when the terrifying motive of the Marquis de Bressac's seductions was at last presented to me in all its horror. We were at that time residing in the country and I was attending the Comtesse alone, her first maid having obtained leave to remain in Paris for the summer owing to some business of her husband. One evening, shortly after I had withdrawn from my mistress, and not being able, because of the extreme heat, to think of going to bed, I was taking the air on a balcony giving on to my room. Suddenly the Marquis knocked at my door, begging me to let him speak with me for a while . . . Alas, every moment granted me by this cruel author of my woes seemed so precious that I never dared to refuse him a single one. He entered, closed the door with care, and threw himself into an armchair facing me.

'Listen to me, Sophie,' he said with a little embarrassment, 'I have things of the greatest importance to confide in you – but I must ask you to swear that you will never reveal anything of what I am about to speak.'

'Oh, Monsieur, could you possibly believe me capable of abusing your confidence?'

'You do not know what you would risk if ever you should prove to me that I had been deceived in trusting you!'

'The greatest of my sorrows would be the loss of your confidence – there is no need to threaten me with anything worse.'

'Very well, Sophie . . . I have decided that my mother's life must be cut short, and yours is the hand I have chosen to help me in this conspiracy.'

'You have chosen me, Monsieur!' I cried, recoiling in horror; 'in Heaven's name how could two such schemes have entered your mind? Take my life, Monsieur; it is yours to dispose of as you will – in fact I owe it to you; but do not hope to obtain any assistance from me in a crime even the idea of which is intolerable to my heart.'

'Listen, Sophie,' said Monsieur de Bressac, quietly trying to calm me down; 'I am well aware of your repugnance in these matters; but, as you are intelligent, I flatter myself that I may overcome your objections by making you see that this crime, which you find so enormous, is really at bottom a very simple thing. Two hideous actions confront your unphilosophic eyes: the destruction of a creature like to ourselves, and the augmentation of the evil arising from the fact that this creature happens to be my mother. As far as the destruction of one's kind is concerned, you may be certain, Sophie, that such a belief is entirely chimerical, since the power of destruction has not been accorded to man. At the very most he has the ability of causing things to change form – but he cannot annihilate them. Moreover all forms are equal in the eyes of nature; and nothing is lost in the immense crucible wherein her variations are achieved. All the particles of matter thrown therein incessantly renew themselves under other shapes; and whatever effect our individual actions may have upon this process, none directly injure it, none outrage it. Our destructions reanimate its power and conserve its energy, but they never weaken it.

'And of what importance is it to eternally creative nature if this mass of flesh which today presents the shape of a woman should tomorrow reproduce itself in the guise of a thousand different insects? Would you dare to claim that the construction of individuals such as we costs more effort than the construction of a worm, and that she ought, in consequence, to take a greater interest in us? But if the degree of attachment, or rather of indifference, is the same, what can it matter to her if, by means of what we call crime, a man causes another human being to change into a fly or a lettuce? When the sublimity of our species has been proved to me, when it has been demonstrated to me that we are so important in nature's eyes that her laws are incensed at our destruction – then I shall be able to believe that this destruction is a crime. But when the most deliberate study of nature has proved to me that everything which vegetates on this earth, everything that reproduces, including even the most imperfect of her works, are all of equal value in her eyes, I shall never be able to believe that the transformation of one of these creatures into a thousand others could possibly offend her laws. Rather should I say to myself: all men, plants, and animals grow and mature, reproduce themselves and destroy themselves by similar means; but they never really die – all they do is to undergo a simple variation which modifies their substance. Every one of them might, I say, advance themselves in life, one against another, destroy themselves, procreate indifferently and without discrimination, appear one moment in one form, and another moment in another – they might even, at the whim of the being who wished or was able to transform them, change thousands of times during the course of a day without a single law of nature being for even the slightest fraction of a second affected.

'But this being whom I attack happens to be my mother, she who carried me in her womb! What of it? Should such an empty consideration prevent me? And has it any right to do so? Was she thinking of me, this mother you speak of, when in a fit of lubricity she conceived the foetus which grew into the man I am? Do I owe any duty to her because she occupied herself with her own pleasure? In any case it isn't the mother's blood which forms the child, but only that of the father. The female breast nourishes, maintains, and helps build the child, but in reality it furnishes nothing. It is this thought which would never have allowed me to shorten my father's days, but which shows me what a very simple thing it would be to cut the thread of my mother's. Nevertheless, I admit the possibility that the heart of a child may be moved – quite justly – with some feelings of gratitude towards its mother; but we experience such emotions only on the basis of her actions and behaviour towards us throughout our childhood. If she has behaved well we may love her, perhaps we even ought to do so. If, on the other hand, she has acted towards us in an evil way, we are not only bound by no law of nature, but we owe her nothing at all. Under such circumstances the vigorous power of the ego – which naturally and invincibly persuades a man to disembarrass himself of everything which he finds harmful or injurious – this vigorous power, I say, resolves our decision to get rid of such a woman.'

'Oh, Monsieur,' I replied, absolutely appalled by such reasoning, 'the indifference you suppose to be inherent in nature is, in reality, nothing but the work of your passions. Condescend for an instant to listen to your heart instead of your intellectual reasonings, and you will see how it condemns the imperious suggestions stimulated by your libertinism. This heart to whose tribunal I beg you to appeal, is it not the sanctuary wherein that nature, whom you so frequently attack, begs us to listen to and respect her? If you discover that she has inscribed therein the most absolute horror for such a crime as you meditate, will you not agree with me that it should be condemned? If you reply that the fire of your passions destroys this horror within a second, then I wish to impress on you the fact that no sooner will you be satisfied than it shall quickly be reborn, making itself felt through the all-powerful emotion of remorse.

'The greater your sensitivity, the more quickly will its power tear you to pieces . . . Each day, each minute, you shall see her before your eyes, this tender mother whom your barbarous band has cast into the tomb. You shall hear her plaintive voice repeatedly pronouncing the sweet name which brought such delight into your childhood. She will haunt your wakeful nights, torment your dreams, opening with her bloody hands the wounds with which you tore her body. From then on not a happy moment shall shine for you on this earth: all your pleasures will be poisoned, all your thoughts will be troubled; and a celestial hand, whose power you deny, will avenge the days of the mother you have destroyed by poisoning all your own. Without having derived any pleasure from your crimes you will perish from the fatal regret of having dared to carry them out.'

I was in tears while pronouncing these last words, and throwing myself at the knees of the Marquis I conjured him by all that he held most dear to forget such infamous aberrations, swearing I would hide his revelation of them for the remainder of my life. But I did not know the heart I sought to soften. Whatever moral force he may have had, crime had abated its strength; and the passions, in all their furious ardour, permitted none but criminal ideas to reign in his breast.

The Marquis got up coldly: 'I see well enough that I have allowed myself to be deceived, Sophie,' he said; 'I am almost as sorry about it for your sake as for mine. But it doesn't matter – I shall find other means for achieving my aims; and you'll find you've lost a great deal through not helping me, while your mistress will gain nothing by it.'

This menacing attitude changed all my ideas. In not accepting complicity in the crime he proposed I was opening myself to very considerable risk, and my mistress would still undoubtedly perish. In consenting to his request I would be shielding myself from the wrath of my young master, and would eventually be able to save his mother. This reflection, which passed through my mind within the space of a split second, immediately persuaded me to change my role. But as such a retraction of sentiment would have appeared unduly suspicious, I cautiously postponed my defeat by the sophisms of the Marquis, and gave him, instead, plenty of opportunity to repeat them. Little by little I assumed the air of not knowing how to reply to them – and he believed me vanquished. I accounted for my change of heart as being due to the power of his arguments, and eventually pretended to accept everything he proposed. Suddenly I felt the lips of the Marquis pressed against my neck . . . How this movement would have overwhelmed me with joy had not these barbarous projects annihilated every loving sentiment which my indulgent heart had dared to conceive for him . . . Ah! If it had only been possible that I might still love him . . .

'You are the first woman I have ever embraced,' exclaimed the Marquis, 'and, truly, it is with all my heart! You are delightful, my child! It seems that a ray of philosophy must have penetrated your spirit. Is it really possible that this charming head should have remained so long in the shadows?'

And the next moment we were planning our crime. But in order that the Marquis should the more easily fall into my trap, I retained a certain air of repugnance as he explained each additional detail in the development of his project. It was this pretence, so permissible in my desperate situation, which succeeded better than anything else in deceiving my companion. It was decided that in approximately two or three days – depending on how the opportunity presented itself – I should skilfully empty a little packet of poison, given me by the Marquis, into the usual morning cup of chocolate served to the Comtesse. Monsieur de Bressac guaranteed the success of the remainder of the intrigue, and promised me an income of two thousand crowns, adding that I might spend the remainder of my days either under his roof or wherever else might seem suitable to me. He made this promise without indicating the precise circumstances in which I was to enjoy such a favour, and we parted.

Meanwhile something so peculiar happened, something so indicative of the character of the atrocious young man with whom I was involved, that I really must remark on it. Two days after our conversation the Marquis received the news that an uncle, of whom he never expected to be the heir, had died and left him a fortune of eighty thousand livres.

'Gracious heaven!' I exclaimed to myself when I heard this. 'Is it in this manner that celestial justice punishes the plottings of criminals? Here I am, almost having lost my life for refusing much inferior sums, and yet this nobleman has been placed at the pinnacle of wealth and good fortune after having conceived the most terrifying of crimes.'

But quickly repenting of this blasphemy against providence I sank to my knees, begging pardon of God and feeling that this unexpected inheritance might at least change the plans of the Marquis . . . My God! – how considerable was my error!

'My dear Sophie,' said Monsieur de Bressac, coming into my room that same evening, 'prosperity rains down on me! I have told you twenty times, there is nothing like a preoccupation with crime for attracting good fortune. In fact it would seem that her path is only opened easily to evildoers. Eighty and sixty, my child – together they make one hundred and forty livres of income for the service of my pleasures.'

'Then, sir,' I replied, with a surprise moderated by the circumstances in which I was placed, 'this unexpected wealth hasn't decided you in favour of waiting patiently for the death of the lady whose departure you wished to hasten?'

'Wait? – I shan't wait two minutes, my child! Can't you realise I'm twenty-eight, and that at my age it is extremely hard to have to wait! I beg you not to think that this could change any of our projects. Let us have the consolation of bringing all this business to a close before we return to Paris . . . Try and make it tomorrow – or the day after at the latest. I'm looking forward to giving you the first instalment of your pension.'

I did my best to disguise the dismay with which this rabid obsession with crime filled me, and reassumed my role of the previous day. But my feelings were almost numb and my only sensation was one of horror for such a hard and profligate wretch.

No position could have been more awkward than that in which I now found myself. If I didn't play my agreed part the Marquis would quickly come to the conclusion that I was making a fool of him; if I warned Madame de Bressac, whatever steps such a revelation might cause her to take the young man would realise he had been hoaxed, and would very soon decide on more sure means of despatching his mother to another world – and at the same time I should be exposed to all the fury of his vengeance. The only way remaining open to me was that of the law; but not for anything in the world would I have consented to take it. I therefore determined that, whatever might happen, it was essential to warn the Comtesse.

'Madame,' I said to her, the day after my conversation with the Marquis, 'I have something of the greatest importance to disclose to you. Yet, despite the fact that it is urgent and serious and concerns you intimately, I have decided to guard my silence unless you can give me your word of honour never to show any sign of resentment towards your son for what he has had the audacity to plan. You will act as you think fit, Madame; you will take whatever seems the best course open to you, but you will never reveal a word of what I have told you. I must ask you to promise me this, for otherwise I can say nothing to you.'

Madame de Bressac, who thought it was merely something to do with her son's usual extravagant behaviour, promised all I asked. And then I acquainted her with all the facts. The unhappy woman burst into tears on learning of her son's infamy.

'The unholy wretch,' she cried, ' – what have I ever done, except it were for his good? If I tried to prevent his indulgence in vice, or to correct him, what motive other than that of his happiness and peace could ever have led me to be severe with him? To what does he owe the inheritance which has recently fallen to him, if not to my efforts? If I have hidden from him my part in the matter it was simply to spare his feelings . . . The monster! Oh, Sophie, give me proof of his evil schemes, put me into such a position that I shall no longer be able to doubt them! I need every scrap of evidence that can extinguish the natural maternal sentiment still present in my heart . . . '

So I showed the Comtesse the packet of poison which had been given me. We gave a small dose to a dog and carefully shut him up. Within two hours it died in the most terrible convulsions. The Comtesse, no longer being able to doubt, decided immediately on the course she must take. Taking possession of the remainder of the poison, she instantly despatched a courier, bearing a letter, to her kinsman, the Duc de Sonzeval, begging him to go speedily and secretly to the Minister to explain the terrible crime of which she was about to become victim, and to procure a *lettre de cachet* for the imprisonment of her son. In short, he was to save her as quickly as possible from the monster who planned to kill her . . . Nevertheless, by some inconceivable dispensation of heaven this abominable crime was to be consummated.

The discovery of the unhappy dog who had served for our experiment was clear enough indication to the Marquis as to precisely what had happened. He heard it howling, and knowing that it was specially beloved of his mother, made urgent enquiry as to what was wrong with it, and where it was. Those whom he questioned were ignorant of the facts, and thus could not reply. But, doubtless, from that moment, suspicions began to form in his mind. He said nothing but I could see that he was worried, agitated, and on the watch throughout the day. I kept the Comtesse informed, but no further steps could be taken; all that it was possible to do was to hasten the courier and conceal the object of his mission. Therefore Madame de Bressac told her son that she was hurriedly sending to Paris to beg the Duc de Sonzeval to get in touch immediately with the administrators of the uncle whose heir he had just become, for if someone did not appear soon there might be lawsuits to fear. She added that she had asked the Duc to come and give her an account of the precise details so that, if necessary, she could put in an appearance herself, accompanied by her son. The Marquis, who was too good a physiognomist not to notice the anguish on his mother's face and the confusion on my own appeared to be satisfied by the explanation; but was careful at the same time to be the more surely on his guard. Under the pretext of going on a walking party with his minions, he left the castle and waited in ambush for the messenger at a spot which the man was obliged to pass. And the courier, much more devoted to the son than to the mother, made no ado whatever about handing over his mail. Whereon the Marquis, convinced of what he undoubtedly called my treachery, presented him with a hundred louis, ordering him never again to show his face at the castle. Then he returned home burning with rage, but did his best to control himself. When he met me he joked as usual, and asked if tomorrow would be the day, observing that it was essential that the deed should be done before the arrival of the Duc. After which he went quietly to bed without giving himself away in the slightest.

If this terrible crime was committed, as the Marquis soon informed me it had been, then it could only have been done in the following way . . . Madame took her chocolate the next morning according to her habit, and as it had passed only through my hands I can be certain that it had not been tampered with. But about ten o'clock the Marquis entered the kitchen, and finding only the cook present he ordered him to go at once and get some peaches from the garden. The cook expostulated that it was impossible to leave his work, yet the Marquis insisted on his craving for peaches and said he would keep an eye on the stove. So the cook went out and Monsieur de Bressac examined all the dishes prepared for dinner. He seemingly mixed the fatal drug which was to end his mother's days with some white-beet salad – of which she was passionately fond. When dinner was served, the Comtesse doubtless partook of this sinister dish. These are merely my own suspicions, but it was obviously by some such means that the crime was accomplished. Monsieur de Bressac assured me, in the unfortunate sequel to this adventure, that his blow had been struck, and that my collusion with the victim had simply offered him an alternative means for the success of his intentions. But let us leave these horrible conjectures and come to the cruel manner in which I was punished for not having wished to participate in this terrifying business, as well as for my having revealed the nature of the plot . . .

On arising from the meal I have just indicated the Marquis came up to me: 'Listen, Sophie,' he said, with all the appearance of phlegmatic calm, 'I have found a more certain means for concluding my plans than that which I originally proposed to you. But it needs to be discussed in detail. I dare not continue coming so frequently to your room, for I fear the eyes of everyone. At five o'clock precisely be at the corner of the park. I shall meet you, and while we take a long walk together I shall explain everything.'

I cannot but admit that, whether it was by a dispensation of providence owing to excessive innocence, or simply to blindness, nothing caused me to anticipate the fearful ordeal which awaited me. I was so confident of the secrecy of the arrangements I had made with the Comtesse that I never imagined that the Marquis would be able to uncover them. Nevertheless I felt some embarrassment in the matter.

Perjury is a virtue when it promises crime

– so wrote one of our tragic poets. But perjury is always odious for the delicate and sensitive soul which finds itself obliged to have recourse to it. Thus I found my role awkward – but it was not to be for long. The detestable proceedings of the Marquis, while giving me other causes for pain, soon set my mind at rest regarding that particular embarrassment. He came up to me with the gayest air and the most open attitude in the world: and side by side we advanced together into the forest without him doing anything other than laughing and joking, as was his custom with me. When I wished to turn the conversation towards the object for which he had arranged this meeting, he kept telling me to wait, explaining that he feared we might be observed as we were not yet in safety. Imperceptibly we arrived at the thicket and the great oak where he first encountered me. I could not help shuddering at seeing these again. My imprudence and all the horror of my fate seemed to rise before my eyes with terrible intensity. And you can judge how my terror redoubled itself when I saw at the foot of that gloomy tree, two young minions of the Marquis considered to be those he loved most. They got up as we approached and threw on to the grass a collection of ropes, lashes and other instruments which made me tremble.

Then the Marquis dropped his previous manner and began to abuse me with the grossest and most horrible of insults: 'Bitch!' he exclaimed, even before we were within hearing distance of the young men, 'do you remember this thicket from which I brought you like some savage beast – to restore you to a life which you deserved only to lose? Do you recognise that tree whereon I threatened to lash you again, if ever you gave me cause to repent of my bounty? Why did you accept the services I asked of you against my mother if you intended to betray me? And how did you imagine you were serving virtue when you were risking the liberty of the man to whom you owed your life? Unavoidably faced with a choice between two crimes, why did you choose the most abominable? You had only to refuse what I asked of you, instead of accepting it, in order to betray me!'

Then the Marquis acquainted me with all he had done to waylay the courier, and the nature of the suspicions which had caused him to make such a decision.

'What have you achieved by your falseness, unworthy slut?' he continued. 'You have risked your own life without saving my mother's, for the blow has already fallen, and I hope on my return to see my success amply crowned. But first I must punish you; I must teach you that the path of virtue is not always the best, and that there are situations in life where complicity in crime is preferable to the role of informer. Knowing me as you do, how have you dared deceive me? Did you think that the sentiment of pity – a sentiment which my heart never admits except in the interest of my pleasures – or a few religious precepts, such as I constantly trample underfoot, would be capable of restraining me? . . . Or perhaps you were counting on your charms?'

He added these words in the most cruel and bantering tone . . .

'Very well then! I am going to prove to you that these charms, made as naked as it is possible to make them, will serve only to inflame my vengeance the more . . . '

And without giving me time to reply, without giving the slightest proof of emotion at the torrent of tears which overwhelmed me, he seized me brutally by the arm and dragged me to his satellites.

'Here,' he said to them, 'is the woman who wished to poison my mother, and who perhaps already has committed this shocking crime, despite my attempts to prevent her. I should perhaps have placed her in the hands of the law; but then she would have lost her life and it is my wish that she should retain it so that she shall have a much longer time in which to suffer. Strip her quickly of her clothes and tie her with her belly against this tree so that I may chastise her in the manner she deserves.'

The order was no sooner given than it was fulfilled. Making me embrace the tree as closely as possible, they tied a handkerchief around my mouth and bound me to it by my shoulders and legs, leaving the remainder of my body free, so that nothing should come between my flesh and the blows it was to receive. The Marquis, agitated to an astonishing extent, seized one of the lashes. But before he struck me the inhuman devil closely observed my face. You might have said that he feasted his eyes on my tears and the marks of pain and dismay which impregnated my every feature . . . Then he moved behind me to a distance of about three feet, and I suddenly felt myself struck with all possible force from the middle of my back down to my very calves. My butcher then stopped for a minute and brutally touched all the parts he had mangled . . . I do not know what he whispered to one of his satellites, but within a second my head was covered with a handkerchief which no longer left me the slightest possibility of observing any of their movements. There was, in fact, a considerable amount of motion behind me before the resumption of the further bloody scenes to which I was destined . . . 'Yes! Good – that's it!' exclaimed the Marquis before he lashed me again. And hardly had these incomprehensible words been pronounced than the blows rained down with even greater violence. There was another pause. Once more the hands moved over the lacerated portions of my body, to be followed by further whispering. Then one of the young men said aloud: 'Am I not better thus?' These new words were equally mysterious to me, but the Marquis only replied: 'Get nearer, get nearer!' A third attack followed, still more brutal than those that had gone before, and during which Bressac exclaimed repeatedly, mingling his words with terrifying oaths: 'Go on then, go on, both of you – can't you see that I wish to make her die on the spot, and beneath my very hand!' These words, gradually pronounced louder, terminated this infamous butchery. Once again the men spoke softly together for several minutes. This was followed by more movement, and then I felt the cords which bound me being loosened. The grass, covered with my blood, showed me the state I must be in. The Marquis was alone; his assistants had vanished . . .

'Very well, you bitch,' he said, looking at me with the kind of expression which follows the delirium of the passions, 'don't you find virtue rather expensive, and that a pension of two thousand crowns was preferable to a hundred strokes with a lash?'

I threw myself at the foot of the tree, almost ready to lose consciousness . . . The lecherous fiend, not yet satisfied by the horrors he had just indulged and cruelly excited by the sight of my wounds, trampled me beneath his feet, and so crushed me against the ground that I was almost suffocated.

'It is more than good of me to have spared your life,' he repeated two or three times. 'So at least be careful as to what use you make of this new indulgence of mine . . . '

Then he ordered me to get up and clothe myself. As blood was flowing everywhere I mechanically gathered some grass to dry myself, for I did not wish that my garments – the only ones I had – should be stained. Meanwhile the Marquis walked to and fro, leaving me alone, for he was more concerned with his thoughts than with his victim. The swelling of my flesh, the blood which still continued to flow, and the frightful pain I was enduring, all these things combined to render the movements necessary in dressing a virtual impossibility. But not once did this ferocious man, this monster who was responsible for my cruel condition – he for whom a few days previously I would have given my very life – not once was he moved by the slightest feeling of that commiseration which might have urged him to help me.

When I was dressed he approached me: 'You may go where you wish,' he said. 'You must have some money in your pocket, so I shan't deprive you of it. But take care never to appear near my establishments again – either at Paris or here in the country. I am warning you now that you will be publicly known as the murderess of my mother. If she is still breathing when I return home I shall see that she carries this idea with her into the grave. The whole house shall know it, and I am going to denounce you officially before the law. Therefore you will find Paris even more uninhabitable than before; for I must inform you that your first difficulty there, which you thought ended, was merely hushed up. You were told that it was erased from the records – but in that you were deceived. You were left in this situation in order that your subsequent behaviour might be observed. So now you have two trials to face instead of one. And in place of a vile usurer as your adversary, you have a rich and powerful man, a man who is determined to pursue you as far as the very gates of hell – should you, by way of slander or calumny, abuse the life he so generously leaves you.'

'Oh, sir!' I replied, 'however severe you may have been towards me, do not fear that I shall take any steps against you. I felt it was my duty to interfere where your mother's life was concerned, but I should never attempt to contradict you when it is only a question of the unfortunate Sophie. Adieu, Monsieur, and may your crimes render you as happy as your cruelties have tortured me. And whatever destiny heaven may have in store for you, so long as it shall spare my lamentable days I shall employ them only in imploring its mercy on you.'

The Marquis raised his head. As I spoke these words he could not help looking at me; and seeing me all wet with tears, scarcely able to support myself, the cruel man, doubtless in fear of being moved to pity, turned away. When he had disappeared I let myself fall to the ground, abandoning myself to all the intensity of my pain. The air around re-echoed with my sobs, and I watered the grass with my tears. 'Oh, God,' I cried. 'You have willed it. It was by Your decree that the innocent should once more become the prey of the guilty. Dispose of me as you will, Father, for I am yet far from the evils which You have suffered for us. Grant that those I endure while adoring You may render me worthy, one day, of those recompenses You have promised the weak – the weak who always keep You in mind in their tribulations, and who glorify You in their anguish!'

Night came, but I was in no state to travel far. Though scarcely able to stand I remembered the thicket where I had slept four years before, though in a much less miserable condition. I dragged myself to it as best I could; and lying on the same spot, tormented by my still bleeding wounds and overcome by the sufferings of my spirit and the ache in my heart, I passed the cruellest night anyone could possibly imagine. The vigour natural to my age and temperament having given me a little strength by daybreak, and too scared to remain where I was in the neighbourhood of that cruel castle, I quickly left the forest determined, whatever the difficulties, to reach the first dwellings I should come upon. At length I reached the town of Claye, situated about six leagues from Paris. I asked for the surgeon's house and someone pointed it out to me. I implored this gentleman to dress my wounds, telling him that I had fled my mother's house in Paris because of a disappointment in love, and that as my way unfortunately led me through the forest of Bondy I had fallen amongst thieves who had treated me as he could see. He attended to me on condition that I made a deposition to the clerk of the local court. I consented. Probably they made some investigations, but I never heard speak of them. As for the surgeon, he insisted that I stayed with him until I had recovered, and he looked after me with such art that in less than a month I had completely recovered.

As soon as my condition permitted me to go out of doors my first preoccupation was to find some young village girl careful enough and sensible enough to be able to visit the Château de Bressac, so that she might discover everything that had happened there since my departure. Curiosity was not the only motive which determined me in this proceeding. In fact such a desire for information might have been dangerous and would certainly have been unsuited to my circumstances, but I had left in my room the little money I had earned while working for the Comtesse and I had barely six louis with me – although I had nearly thirty at the Château. I did not imagine that the Marquis could be cruel enough to refuse me what was legitimately mine, and I was convinced that once fury was over he would not burden me with a second injustice. So I wrote him a letter in terms as touching as I could find . . . It seemed, alas, that I overdid matters. My sad heart somehow still spoke in favour of this perfidious man. I carefully hid from him my present whereabouts, and begged him to send me my personal effects and the little money which belonged to me. A peasant girl of twenty or twenty-five years, very bright and wide-awake, promised to deliver my letter and to make enough discreet enquiries to be able to satisfy me on her return regarding the various matters about which I was anxious. I expressly advised her not to disclose where she came from, nor yet to speak of me at all; but to say that she had been given the letter by a man who had brought it over a distance of more than fifteen leagues. Jeannette – for that was the name of my messenger – set off for the Château and returned with my reply within twenty-four hours. But first, Madame, it is essential that I acquaint you with all that had happened at the Bressac estate before I tell you the contents of the letter.

The Comtesse de Bressac fell grievously ill the day of my departure from her home, and she died suddenly that same night. Nobody arrived from Paris, and the Marquis, in the depths of despair (the hypocrite!), pretended that his mother had been poisoned by a chambermaid named Sophie, who had escaped the same day. A search was being made for this servant and, if discovered, she was to die on the scaffold. The Marquis, however, had found that his inheritance had made him even richer than he expected. The contents of the strongboxes, the jewels of Madame de Bressac, and various items which had not been considered – all these, in addition to his other revenues, put the young man in possession of more than six hundred thousand francs in goods and cash. It was said that, beneath his affectation of grief, he experienced considerable difficulty in hiding his joy. Those kinsmen whom he had summoned to be present at the autopsy had deplored the end of the unhappy Comtesse, swearing to avenge her should she who had committed such a crime fall into their hands; and then they left the young man in full and peaceful possession of the fruits of his treachery. Monsieur de Bressac had spoken to Jeannette himself, asking her various questions, to which the young woman replied with such firmness and intrepidity that he decided to satisfy her demands without pressing her further.

'Here is the fatal letter,' said Sophie, bringing it from her pocket. 'I shall keep it until my last breath, Madame. Take it, read it if you can, without shuddering!'

Madame de Lorsange, having taken the note from the hands of our beautiful adventuress, read therein the following words:

A wretch capable of having poisoned my mother is unusually bold in daring to write me after such an execrable crime. The best thing for her to do is to see to it that she covers her tracks as well as she can, for she may be certain that she will pay for it if she is found. What does she dare to claim? . . . What does she say about money and personal effects? Does what she left behind equal in amount the total of her thefts during her stay in my house? Does it compensate in the slightest for her latest crime? She had better avoid sending me a second envoy with another letter like to her first – for such a messenger will be kept under restraint until the whereabouts of the guilty woman have officially been made known to justice.

'Continue, my dear child,' said Madame de Lorsange as she returned the note to Sophie. 'Such behaviour is most disgusting; especially in one who, rolling in wealth, refuses her honestly earned wages to an unfortunate creature who did not wish to concur in a crime. Such infamy, in fact, seems to me without precedent.'

'Alas, Madame,' continued Sophie, as she took up the sequel of her tale, 'I wept for two days over this wretched letter; and I sobbed more over the horrible possibilities it suggested than over the refusal it contained.

'So I am guilty!' I cried. 'So I must a second time be denounced before the law for having rigidly observed its decrees . . . Let it be so, for I repent of nothing I have done. Whatever may happen to me I shall never know either pain or remorse within my own soul so long as I retain its purity. And I shall have the satisfaction of knowing that I have committed no fault other than that of having lent too willing an ear to those whisperings of justice and virtue which will never desert me.'

I nevertheless found it impossible to believe that the searches of which the Marquis had spoken were genuine. There was little to commend their reality, since it would be dangerous for him to have me appear before a court; and I felt certain that he would feel much more terrified of my presence, if ever he should discover me near him, than I need feel of his threats. These reflections decided me on staying where I was and to obtain some work, if I could, until slightly increased funds would allow me to move on.

I communicated my project to Rodin, which was the name of the surgeon at whose house I was staying. He approved, and even proposed that I continue my residence with him. But before I tell you what happened to me there it is necessary that I should give you an idea of this man and those who made up his household.

Rodin was a man of forty, with dark and heavy eyebrows, a quick penetrating glance and a strong and healthy form. His features and manner seemed to indicate a libertine temperament. Possessed of an income of between ten and twelve thousand livres a year, Rodin exercised the surgical art only from taste. He lived in a very fine house which, since his wife had died several years previously, he occupied with two servant girls to wait on him and his daughter, Rosalie, who had just attained her fourteenth year. This lovely girl united all the charms best calculated to cause delight; her waist was nymph-like, her face round, fresh, with extraordinary animation. She had delicate and pleasing features, the prettiest mouth possible, large black eyes which reflected her goodness of soul and shone with sentiment, chestnut coloured hair, which fell round her shoulders, skin of an incredible and dazzling smoothness, and the loveliest bosom in the world. She was possessed, moreover, of the wit and liveliness of one of the fairest souls that nature had as yet created. As for the maidservants with whom I was to serve in this house, both were peasants. One was governess and the other cook. The first was about twenty-five years old, and the other between eighteen and twenty. Both were extremely pretty, and such a choice gave me reason to suspect the eagerness which Rodin displayed in engaging me. 'What need has he of a third woman?' I asked myself; 'and why does he want them so good-looking? Assuredly,' I continued, 'there is something in all this which doesn't conform to that conventional and regular behaviour from which I never wish to stray. The matter, therefore, needs careful investigation.'

Consequently I begged Monsieur Rodin to allow me to convalesce in his house for one more week, assuring him that before the end of that time he would receive my decision on what he wished to propose to me.

I profited by this interval to become more closely acquainted with Rosalie, determined not to settle with her father if there were any circumstances in his house likely to offend me. With this view in mind I kept a close watch on everything, and the following day noticed that this man had an arrangement which, from the start, aroused in me the most violent suspicions regarding his conduct.

Rodin kept in his home a school for children of both sexes. He had obtained an official permit to do so during the lifetime of his wife, and the authorities had felt themselves unable to deprive him of it once he had lost her. His pupils were not numerous, but they were carefully chosen; and he had, in all, only fourteen girls and fourteen boys. He would never accept them below the age of twelve, and they were obliged to leave as soon as they had reached sixteen. I have rarely seen young people so handsome as those received into this establishment. And whenever this man was faced with a boy or girl showing either bodily defect or lack of good features, he would tactfully refuse them admittance under twenty different pretexts, all tinged with sophisms to which nobody could reply. Thus, however small, his little group of boarders were always beautiful and always charming. I had not seen this little group previously because, arriving during the holidays, the scholars were all absent. They reappeared towards the time of my recovery.

Rodin supervised the school, the governess teaching the girls until he had finished instructing the boys, at which time he would move into her classroom and take over. He taught his young pupils writing, arithmetic, a little history, drawing, and music – without employing any masters other than himself.

I expressed my astonishment to Rosalie that her father, while exercising the art of surgery, could, at the same time, discharge that of schoolmaster. I also confided my opinion that it appeared strange that a man who was wealthy enough to live at his ease without having need to follow either profession should put himself to so much trouble in order to organise them. Rosalie, with whom by this time I was very friendly, burst into laughter on hearing my remarks. Her manner of receiving my observations only excited my curiosity the more, and I implored her to explain why she reacted so.

'Listen,' explained this charming girl, with all the candour of her age and all the innocence of her amiable character; 'listen, Sophie, I am going to tell you everything, for I can see that you are an honest girl . . . incapable of betraying the secret I am about to confide in you.

'My father is certainly all that you have said of him; and if he exercises both the one and the other profession, as you see him doing, then he has two motives the nature of which I am going to disclose to you. He practices surgery because he likes it, and for the pleasure of making new discoveries – of which he has made many. In fact he has written works so learned that he generally passes for the most skilful and expert man in his field at the present time. He worked twenty years in Paris before he retired to this part of the country, so the real local surgeon is a man named Rombeau, whom my father took under his protection, and with whom he is associated in his experiments. And would you like to know what entices him to run a school? . . . Libertinism, my child, sheer libertinism, a passion which he carries to the extreme. My father finds in his pupils – of both sexes – subjects whom dependence on him makes submissive to his will, and he profits by it . . . But listen! – follow me,' continued Rosalie, 'today is Friday, one of the three days in the week when he corrects those who have been guilty of making mistakes; and it is in this kind of correction that my father finds his delight. Come on, follow me and you shall see how he does it. We can secretly observe everything from a hiding place in my room. But take good care never to reveal a word of what I have told you or of what you are about to see with your own eyes.'

It was so important for me to know the habits of the man who was offering me asylum that I neglected nothing which might help reveal his true nature to me. I followed behind Rosalie and she placed me close to a partition wall in which there were several cracks, sufficiently large to enable us to see everything that happened in the neighbouring room.

We had scarcely taken up our positions when Rodin entered the larger room leading by the hand a young girl of fourteen, fair and beautiful as Love herself. The poor creature was weeping bitterly and seemed, unfortunately, to be only too well acquainted with what was awaiting her. Sobbing, she threw herself at his feet, imploring his pardon. But Rodin, inflexible, seemed to draw from these demonstrations the first sparks of his pleasure – a pleasure which was already sprouting in his heart, signalling itself in his sinister glance . . .

'Oh, no, no,' he cried; 'this has already happened too often, Julie, and I repent of my good nature. It has served only to plunge you into additional faults. Can you imagine that the gravity of this one leaves me any room for clemency? . . . You passed a note to a boy as he came into class, didn't you?'

'Monsieur, I protest that I didn't!'

'Oh! But I saw you, I saw you!'

'Don't believe a word of it,' exclaimed Rosalie. 'These are faults he concocts to bolster up the pretexts for his actions. This little creature is an angel, and it is because she resists him that he treats her so severely.'

During this time Rodin, more and more excited, seized the little girl by the hands and tied them to the top of a post which had been set up in the middle of the 'correction' room, and which was fitted with a ring for this purpose. Julie was thus left with no defence . . . other than her fair head wistfully turned towards her tormenter, her superb hair all dishevelled, and her tears bathing one of the sweetest, most beautiful, and most interesting faces in the world. Rodin gazed on this picture and, inflamed by it, he blindfolded those eyes which sent out such appeals to him. Julie was no longer able to see anything, and Rodin, more at ease, removed the veils of her modesty, raising her chemise as far as her loins, and tucking it up in the edge of her bodice . . . What whiteness, what beauty! Here were roses stripped of their leaves by the very hands of the Graces. What was he, then, this creature who could condemn to torment these charms so fresh and appetising? Who was the monster who could find pleasure in the sight of tears and pain? Rodin surveyed her, his eyes straying everywhere, while his hands dared to profane those flowers which his cruelties were about to stigmatise. As we were directly facing them, no movement escaped us. The libertine continued his lecherous examination until the fury of his lust could no longer be restrained. He first expressed it in invective, menacing her with all manner of threats and evil proposals. The poor little girl began to writhe under the thought of the lashes which she already felt mangling her flesh. Rodin, no longer himself, snatched a fistful of rods from out a great tub of vinegar, where they were steeping to increase their suppleness.

'Come along,' he said, approaching his victim; 'get ready, because you are going to suffer!'

And then this hard-hearted wretch used his vigorous arm to whip the birch plumb-wise across the parts exposed to him. He commenced with twenty-five lashes, which quickly changed to vermilion the tender incarnate of this delicate and tender skin.

Julie screamed, with loud and piercing cries which tore into my soul. Tears flowed beneath the bandage which covered her eyes and fell like pearls on her beautiful cheeks. But all this only roused Rodin to greater fury . . . His hands ran over the parts he had harassed, touched them, pressed them, and seemed to be preparing themselves for new assaults. Rodin recommenced, and every blow was preceded by some invective, a threat, or a reproach . . . The blood flowed . . . Rodin was in ecstasy. He delighted in the contemplation of these visible proofs of his ferocity. He was no longer able to contain himself, and the most indecent of states manifested the fire of his passion. As he made no attempt to hide anything, Julie could see all . . . Indulging in fresh tyrannies he flogged with all the force in his arm. He did not know where to stop. His intoxication reached the pitch of depriving him of any further use of reason. He cursed, he blasphemed, he was ecstatic, and nothing was secure from his barbarous blows. Every piece of flesh before him was treated with the same severity. The wretch stopped, nevertheless, as he wished to postpone his culmination to a later episode.

'Get dressed,' he said to Julie as he untied her; and, readjusting himself, he added: 'and if you do anything similar again don't expect to get off so lightly!'

Julie returned to her classroom while Rodin entered that of the boys. He quickly came back accompanied by a young scholar of fifteen who was beautiful as a summer's day. Rodin grumbled a little, but, more at ease with the boy, joked and kissed him as he lectured him: 'You deserve to be punished,' he exclaimed, 'and you are going to be!'

With these words he seized the child, overleaping all the bounds of modesty. But, contrary to his attitude with the girl, everything interested him here; nothing was excluded, the veils were lifted, and everything was handled or fingered indiscriminately. Rodin threatened, he caressed, he kissed, he indulged in invective. Then his impious fingers sought to awaken in this young boy all the voluptuous sensations which he so urgently felt in himself.

'What have we here!' exclaimed the satyr as he viewed his success; 'just look at you, in the very state which I've expressly forbidden . . .'

Then getting to his feet the hypocrite continued with his upbraiding: 'Ah! but I'm going to punish you for this indecency! You little rogue, you cheat, I must avenge myself for the illusions I have permitted myself to entertain about you!'

The birch was brought out again and Rodin commenced his fustigations. Doubtless more excited than he had been with the little Vestal, his blows became increasingly fierce and increasingly numerous. The child was crying and Rodin was in raptures. But, fresh pleasures calling him, he untied the boy to make way for sacrifices of another kind.

There were further similar episodes with another nine children – five boys and four girls. Horrified by the things I had heard and the scenes I had witnessed, I turned to Rosalie: 'In heaven's name,' I asked, when these frightful tableaux had drawn to a close, 'how can a man give himself up to such excesses? How can he find pleasure in the torments he inflicts?'

'Ah! but you don't know everything yet,' replied Rosalie. 'Listen,' she continued, as she stepped out of the cupboard into her room, 'what you have seen should have made it clear to you that my father takes advantage of the minor misdemeanours of his pupils to indulge his horrors to the utmost. He abuses the young girls in the same manner as he does the boys. In this way the girls are not dishonoured, pregnancy is not to be feared and nothing will prevent them eventually finding husbands. Scarcely a year passes when he doesn't corrupt in this manner almost every boy in the school, and at least half of the other pupils. The two women who serve us are submitted to the same horrors . . . Oh, Sophie,' sobbed Rosalie, as she threw herself into my arms, 'Oh, my dear girl, he has seduced even me, his own daughter, right from the tenderest years of my childhood. I had barely attained my eleventh year when I became his victim . . . I was, alas, without the means of defending myself.'

'But, Madamoiselle,' I interrupted, terrified . . . 'What about religion? At least that way remained open to you . . . Could you not have approached a confessor and told him of your exact circumstances?'

'Ah! You've no idea the extent to which he perverted us, for he stifled in us the slightest sentiment of religion. We were forbidden to attend service, and the little he told me concerning this subject was merely to prevent my ignorance from giving away his impiety. I have never been to confession, and I have never taken my first communion. He even entices his pupils away from religion. As for myself and his behaviour towards me, convince yourself with your own eyes what goes on . . .' And she quickly pushed me back into the cupboard we had recently occupied.

Telling me to remain where I was, Rosalie left me. Shortly afterwards Rodin accompanied his daughter into the room already mentioned, followed by the two women who completed his household. Then this lascivious man, no longer being obliged to keep within limits, abandoned himself freely and without any disguise to all the irregularities debauchery might suggest. The two peasants, both stark naked, were lashed with all the might of his arms, and while he was treating one in this manner the other paid him back in the same coin. During the intervals he loaded with the most immoderate and disgusting caresses his daughter, Rosalie, who was raised up on an armchair. This unfortunate girl was the next to suffer. Rodin fastened her to the post, just as he had fastened Julie; and while his women whipped him – one after the other, and sometimes both together – he lashed his daughter, laying his stripes from the middle of her loins to the lower part of her thighs, and at the same time falling into ecstasies of pleasure. His agitation was extreme. He cursed, shouted, and blasphemed as he whipped . . . Rodin, naked, was in his glory . . . A thousand kisses, each more warm than the rest, gave expression to his ardour . . . Then the bomb exploded, and the pain-intoxicated libertine dared to taste the sweetest of pleasures in the bosom of incest and infamy. At length he felt the need of restoring himself after his exertions. The women were sent away and Rodin went to seat himself at dinner.

Two days after these events he came to my room to ask my reply to his offer. He surprised me in bed. Then, under pretext of seeing if anything remained of the wounds with which I had arrived at his home, he examined me, naked. I was unable to oppose his examining me in this manner, since he had done so twice a day for a month without my ever having perceived in his attitude anything that might offend chastity. But this time Rodin showed signs of other schemes . . . During his observations he passed one of his legs around my loins and pressed it so forcibly that I found myself without defence.

'Sophie,' he said, while his hands wandered round me in such a manner as no longer left me in any doubt, 'you are cured, my dear; and now you are in a position to prove to me the gratitude with which I have already seen your heart filled. Merely this shall be my reward.'

'Monsieur,' I replied, 'I would like to convince you that there is nothing in the whole world which might entice me into the terrible sins you seem to demand of me. I owe you my gratitude, and it is sincerely felt. But I shall not express it at the cost of what is both sin and crime. I am poor and unfortunate, I know, but here is the little money I have.' And with these words I offered him my wretched little purse.

Rodin was confounded by this resistance, which – especially as he knew I was completely without resources – he had so little expected. According to the usual unjust reasoning of men he had expected me to be dishonest and loose simply because I was poor and deserted. He looked at me attentively for a few seconds: 'Sophie,' he commenced, 'it is pretty much out of season to act the Vestal with me. It seems to me that I have some right to your complacency. However,' he sighed, 'keep your money, and do not leave me. I am more than pleased to have such a good girl in my house, for those around me are far from the attainment of virtue. Besides, my daughter loves you, which is a further reason for my begging you to stay . . . '

I accepted his offer. Such a place was worth a fortune to one in my position. Moreover, inflamed with the desire of bringing Rosalie back to the path of goodness and purity, and perhaps of converting her father himself – should I succeed in gaining any influence over him – I did not repent of what I had just done. Rosalie received the news with the greatest transports of joy, and soon I was permanently installed as a member of the household.

Before eight days were over I had commenced working towards the conversions I desired, but the obduracy of Rodin kept spoiling my schemes:

'Do not fancy,' he would reply to my wise counsels, 'that the particular type of homage which I render to your virtue is any proof that I esteem virtue as such, or have any intention of preferring it above vice.

'Do not imagine, Sophie, that anything of the kind is true, for you would merely be deceiving yourself. Those who would interpret my attitude towards you in this sense would be guilty of a considerable error, and it would greatly disturb me if you placed such a construction on what might appear to be my way of thinking. The hut which I use as a shelter when hunting – when the scorching rays of the sun beat too furiously on my body – is neither a beautiful nor a profitable monument. Its necessity is purely one of circumstance: I expose myself to dangers of a kind, I find something which protects me, and naturally I make use of it. But is it any the more useful or profitable for having served its original purpose? Is it any less of a wooden shambles? In a wholly vicious society you would realise that virtue would serve no end whatsoever. But as ours is not that sort of society it becomes necessary to pay lip service to virtue, and to make use of it so that we have less to fear from those who worship its precepts. If nobody adopted it the whole idea would become useless. Thus I am not wrong when I assert that its necessity is only one of opinion or circumstances; virtue is not a type of behaviour of incontestable worth; it is simply a manner of conducting oneself which varies according to climate and race, and which consequently lacks the reality of universal application. The variety of codes in existence, and the fact that laws may be completely changed with equally beneficial results, is sufficient proof of the futility of set virtues and ancient taboos. Only that which is constant is really good, and things which perpetually change cannot pretend to the character of true goodness. That is why immutability has been classed among the perfections of the Eternal. But virtue is wholly devoid of this character – there are not two nations on the face of this globe which are virtuous in the same way; therefore virtue contains nothing real, nothing intrinsically good, and in no way deserves our admiration. It may be necessary to use it as a stay, politically to adopt that of the country in which one happens to live, so as to be left in peace by those who practice it from taste and those who are obliged to reverence it owing to their situation. And again it may be necessary to employ it; because, owing to the respect in which it is held and the preponderance of its conventions, it can guarantee you against the attempts of those who profess vice. Once more, however, all this is simply a matter of circumstance, and nothing in it allows any genuine merit to virtue. There are virtues, moreover, which are impossible for certain men. And how are you going to persuade me that a virtue which combats or denies the passions can truly be found in Nature? And if it cannot be found in Nature, how can it be good? Assuredly you will find, among the men of whom we are speaking, vices opposed to these virtues, and vices which will be preferable, since they represent the only way . . . the only mode of life conforming satisfactorily with their physiological make-up and the functioning of their various organs. According to this hypothesis there must be some very useful vices; so how can virtue claim to be particularly useful, when its contraries can be proved equally so? It has been said that virtue is useful to others, and therefore good; also that if it is only permitted to do to others what is good, I shall thus receive nothing but good in my turn. But such reasoning constitutes a mere sophism. In return for the little good I receive from others – because they practice virtue, and because I am obliged to practice it in my turn – I make a million sacrifices which in no way repay me. Receiving less than I bestow, I consider that I have made a very bad bargain; I experience much more evil from the privations I endure for virtue's sake than the good I receive from those who are described as good. As the arrangement is so unequal, I am unwise to submit to it; and realising that my being virtuous will not bring an amount of good to others equal to the pain and trouble I would experience in forcing myself into their mould, is it not best for me to cease procuring them a happiness which costs me so ill? There remains the wrong I could do others by being vicious, and the evil I will receive in my turn – if everyone is like me. I agree that I am taking a definite risk if I indulge in a wide range of vices; but the chagrin I experience in undertaking such risks is compensated by the pleasure I feel in what I make others risk; thus equality is established and everyone is almost equally happy – which is not, nor could be, the situation in a society in which some are good and others wicked because, from an admixture of this particular type, perpetual snares arise – such as do not exist in a society of the kind I have just suggested. In a mixed society the interests are all diverse, and there we have the source of an infinity of woes. In such a social organisation as I indicated previously, all interests are equal – each individual in the group is endowed with the same tastes, the same propensities, and all march towards the same end. Therefore all are happy. But, fools will tell you, evil does not make a man happy. That may be true when it has been decided to emulate and praise only the good; but depreciate and abase that which you call good and you will revere only that which you once had the folly of calling evil, not because it will be permitted (that would frequently be a reason for the diminishment of its charm), but because the laws, no longer employed for the punishment of crime, would not inspire that fear which reduces the pleasure nature has placed in such actions. I visualise a society in which incest (let us admit this delinquency together with the remainder) is a crime. Those who abandon themselves to it will experience a freezing up of their pleasures, and they will be unhappy – because opinion, law, and religion will all be against them. Those who desire to commit this evil but who are curbed by public opinion from giving way to their desires will equally be unhappy. Thus a law which proscribed incest would only have succeeded in increasing the ranks of unfortunate and unhappy humans. Imagine another society in which incest is not a crime and you will discover that those who do not desire it will not be unhappy, while those who do so will be happy. Therefore a society permitting this act is much more suitable for men than one which raises it to the level of a crime. And the same applies to many other acts wrongly considered as criminal. Examining the state of things from my own viewpoint, I find a crowd of unhappy beings; but immediately I perceive that, by granting them freedom, everyone becomes happy in his own way – and nobody has further cause for complaint. Because under these conditions the man who likes such and such an action delivers himself up to it in peace; and those who do not care for it either remain in a state of indifference (which is in no wise painful) or repay the wrong they may have received by a host of other wrongs which enable them to hurt, in their turn, all those of whom they have cause to complain. Therefore, in a criminal society, people either find themselves very happy or in a state of unconcern which in no wise inconveniences them. Consequently virtue no longer presents the illusion of goodness, nor is it clothed in respectability or indicated as a means of attaining happiness. Those who follow it have no cause to puff themselves with pride when the above kind of homage is all that we can render it – forced, as we are, to do so by the constitution of society as we know it. This supposed quality is purely an affair of circumstance, of convention; and when examined closely we find worship chimerical, without the compensation of its fleeting illusion being any the more attractive.'

Such was the infernal logic of Rodin's unfortunate and passionate nature. But Rosalie, milder and much less corrupted, Rosalie, detesting the horrors to which she was subjected, gave way with greater docility to my teaching. I fervently longed to have her discharge her first duties to religion. For this, however, it would have been necessary to get a priest into the house, as well as into my confidence, and Rodin would never have one of them near him – he held them in absolute horror and contempt, together with the beliefs they professed . . . Nor did he permit Rosalie to leave home unaccompanied. It was thus necessary to await a suitable opportunity. So during this delay I employed myself in instructing my friend, in giving her a taste for virtue. Inspiring her with the love of religion, I unveiled for her the holy dogmas of the Church and tried to help her understand something of its sublime mysteries. Implanting these sentiments deep in her young heart, I succeeded in rendering them indispensable to the happiness of her life. And I was glad.

'Everything follows from this first principle,' I told her, ' – that God exists, that he deserves to be worshipped, and that the most important of the basic elements in this worship is virtue.'

Gradually I taught her other things, and it was not long before Rosalie became a Christian.

Then, quite suddenly, she vanished. Knowing what I did of Rodin, I became most apprehensive as to the fate of this unfortunate girl and immediately resolved to do everything in my power to discover what had happened. The day after her disappearance I thought I heard sobs coming from the direction of a remote cellar. I descended and placed my ear against the door . . . No longer was I in doubt!

'Sophie,' I heard at last, 'Sophie – Oh, Sophie, is it you?'

'Yes, my dearest, my closest friend,' I cried as I recognised the voice of Rosalie . . . 'Yes, it's Sophie whom heaven has sent to rescue you . . . '

And my questions multiplied themselves so rapidly that the poor girl scarcely had a chance of replying. At length I learned that several hours before her disappearance, Rombeau, the friend and colleague of Rodin, had examined her naked; and that she had been ordered by her father to submit to the same horrors with Rombeau as those to which he himself regularly subjected her. She had resisted; but Rodin, furious, had seized her and held her down before the lecherous assaults of his partner. Afterwards the two friends had whispered together for a long time, returning at intervals to examine her afresh, or to maltreat her in a hundred different and criminal fashions. Finally, after a pretence at sending her to stay with a relative, she had been thrown into this cellar where she was well enough fed and cared for.

When her abundant tears had ceased flowing, I asked the poor girl if she knew where they kept the key to this cellar. She didn't know, so I searched everywhere – but without success. Swearing to return the next day I was obliged to leave my dear friend with nothing but my consolation, my assurances of help, and many tears.

That night Rombeau was dining with Rodin. Determined, by any means, to shed some light on the situation of my mistress, I hid myself in a place adjoining the room where the two friends were seated. Their conversation soon convinced me only too well of the horrible project with which both were preoccupied.

'Never will anatomy fully be understood,' said Rodin, 'until the vessels have been examined as they are found in a child of fourteen or fifteen who has died a cruel death. It is only by this means that we can obtain a complete analysis of a part so interesting.'

'It is just the same,' replied Rombeau 'when we come to the membrane which proves virginity. For such an examination a young girl is very necessary. For what does one observe once puberty has been reached? Nothing! The hymen has already been affected and all subsequent researches are inexact. Your daughter is precisely what we need. Although she is fifteen she has not yet attained puberty. And the manner in which we have enjoyed her has not damaged this membrane. Besides, we can study her at our ease. I am absolutely delighted that you have at last determined on this experiment.'

'I am certainly determined,' replied Rodin. 'It is odious for anyone to let futile considerations arrest the progress of science. Have the greatest men ever allowed themselves to be hampered by such contemptible chains? And when Michelangelo wished to represent the figure of Christ realistically, did he make it an issue with his conscience as to whether or not he should crucify a young man so as to copy his anguish and suffering? So far as our own art is concerned, what an urgent need there is for the employment of analogous methods! When it is a case of sacrificing one subject to save a million, should one haggle about the price? Is execution as performed under the law any different from what we are about to do? And the object of this law, which we find so wise – is it not the sacrifice of one individual so that a thousand may be saved?'

As the meal came to a close, the measures proposed by these demented creatures, their actions and preparations, together with the fact that finally they were in a state almost bordering on delirium, all served to show me that not a minute was to be lost – for the unfortunate Rosalie was to be destroyed this same evening. I flew to the cellar, resolved to deliver her or die.

'Oh, my dear friend,' I cried, 'we haven't a moment to lose . . . The monsters . . . They intend to kill you this very night! . . . It won't be long before they are here . . . '

While saying this, I exerted the most violent efforts in an attempt to force the door. One of my pushes caused something to fall. I felt for it with my hand . . . It was the key! Hastily I opened the door, embraced Rosalie, and urged her to flee. She darted out, following close on my steps. Alas, it was still decreed that virtue must fail and that sentiments of the most commiseration should be punished! Rodin and Rombeau, informed by the governess, suddenly appeared. The first seized his daughter just as she cleared the front doorstep. A few more steps and she would have been at liberty!

'Ah! Ah! This is espionage and abduction!' exclaimed Rodin, 'Two of the most dangerous vices in a domestic. Upstairs! Upstairs! We must sit in judgment on this affair!'

Dragged by these two villains, Rosalie and I were brought back to the living quarters and the doors firmly locked. Rodin's unfortunate daughter was tied to the posts of a bed, while all the rage of these furious men was turned on me. I became a butt for the most cruel invective, and the most frightful of sentences was pronounced on me. It was to be nothing less than this: I was to be dissected alive and conscious, so that my heartbeats might be studied whilst I was in that condition. Other observations, impracticable on a corpse, were also to be made on that organ. During this time they stripped me, and I was handled in the most lustful of fashions. Then the blows began to fall and I was so overcome that I dropped unconscious to the ground. Then their rage began to lose something of its vehemence. Rodin brought me round again, and then one of them held me while the other operated. When a toe had been cut from each of my feet they made me sit down, then each pulled a tooth from deep within my mouth.

'That is not all,' said Rodin, as he put an iron in the fire. 'When she came here she had been *whipped*, but I shall send her away *marked.*'

And while his friend held me, the villain applied behind my shoulder the hot iron bearing the mark with which thieves are branded.

'Let her dare, now, to put in an appearance anywhere, the slut!' exclaimed Rodin furiously. 'Having branded her with this ignominious letter I shall sufficiently justify myself for having sent her away with so much secrecy and promptitude.'

Immediately afterwards the two men took hold of me. It was night, and they led me to the edge of the forest where, having warned me of the dangers I risked should I attempt recriminations against them, they cruelly abandoned me.

Many another would have cared little about such a threat. For when I proved that the punishment I had suffered was not by order of any tribunal, what had I to fear? But my weakness, my usual innocence, and the terrible memory of my misfortunes in Paris and at the Château de Bressac all conspired to fill me with misgivings and dismay so that I could think only of getting away from this ominous place as soon as my pains had quietened down a little. As they had carefully dressed the wounds they had inflicted on me, I felt a little better the next day. And having passed, beneath a tree, one of the most frightful nights in my life I set out to walk as soon as daylight appeared. My wounded feet prevented me from moving very quickly; but, anxious to leave the environs of a forest which I found so baleful and sinister, I covered four leagues during that first day and as much again in the two succeeding days. But, never attempting to ascertain my exact whereabouts, and never asking my way, I did little more than continue to circle around the outskirts of Paris. On the fourth day I found myself no further than Lieusaint; yet knowing that this road would lead me towards the southern provinces of France I resolved to follow it, hoping in some way to reach those distant parts. For I imagined that the peace and repose so cruelly refused me in my own part of the country might, perhaps, await me at the other end of the world.

What a fatal error! And what a large amount of trouble was still waiting to test me! My income was much smaller with Rodin than it had been while I was at the Château de Bressac, so it had not been necessary to put a portion of my earnings aside. Thus, luckily, I had them all on my person. They constituted about ten louis – a sum composed of what I had been able to save from my Bressac funds together with what I had been paid at the surgeon's. In the excess of my suffering I still found it possible to be happy that they had left me with this means of support; and I hoped that I would be able to make it last at least until such time as I could find work. The infamies to which I had been subjected did not seem to me to be noticeable. I felt that I would always be able to conceal them, and that their blemishes would not hinder me from earning my living. I was twenty-two, healthy and robust despite my small and slender stature, and my beauty of face, unfortunately, was only too much praised. As for those virtues which up to the moment had always resulted in my injury, they still brought me inward consolation and caused me to hope that providence would eventually bless me, if not with a reward, then at least with a suspension of the evils they had brought upon me.

Filled with hope and courage I continued on my way to Sens. There my imperfectly healed feet caused me to suffer unbearable pain, so I decided to rest for several days. But not daring to trust anyone with the origin of my sufferings, and remembering the names of the drugs I had seen Rodin use for similar wounds, I purchased them and looked after myself. A week of rest restored me completely. It might have been possible to find work at Sens, but urged on by the necessity to go as far as possible I didn't even look for any. I pursued my way with the idea of seeking my fortune in Dauphiné. I had often heard speak of this part of the country when I was a child and therefore imagined that my happiness might lie there. But we shall see how I fared.

In no circumstance of my life has religious sentiment ever abandoned me. Despising the vain sophisms of the brilliant, and looking upon them as manifestations of libertinism as opposed to the utterances of firm conviction, I rejected them with all the force of my conscience and my heart and found, with the aid of one or the other, all that was necessary for reply. I left Auxerre on the seventh of June, and I shall never forget that date. I had travelled about two leagues and the heat was beginning to fatigue me. Ascending a little hill not far from the road – a hill which was crowned with a grove of trees – I lay down beneath their shade to sleep for two or three hours, in this manner refreshing myself at less expense than at an inn – and in greater safety than by the edge of the highway. I climbed up and settled myself at the foot of an oak where, after a frugal lunch consisting of bread and water, I gave myself up to the sweetness of sleep and enjoyed more than two hours of tranquil slumber. When at length I opened my eyes I was delighted with the prospect of the landscape which stretched out below me. From the midst of a forest which stretched far away to the right I thought I beheld – perhaps three or four leagues distant – a small belfry rising modestly into the air.

'Sweet solitude,' I thought to myself, 'how I envy your dwelling-place . . . I suppose that must be the place of retreat of a group of nuns or saintly hermits, occupied only with their own duties and consecrated entirely to religion – people entirely withdrawn from this pernicious society where crime, in her ceaseless war against innocence, always seems to triumph . . . I feel sure that every virtue must dwell in that place.'

I was lost in these thoughts when a young shepherdess about my own age, who tended her sheep on this wooded slope, unexpectedly presented herself to my view. I asked her about the building and she explained that I was looking at a Benedictine monastery occupied by four anchorites who were unequalled in their devotion to religion, chastity, and sobriety.

'People go there once a year,' this girl informed me, 'in order to complete a holy pilgrimage to a miraculous Virgin, from whom pious folk obtain all they can wish.'

Moved by a desire immediately to go and implore succour at the feet of the Holy Mother of God, I asked this young girl if she would like to accompany me. She told me that this was impossible because her mother would be waiting for her at home but that I should not find the way difficult. She pointed it out to me, and told me that I should find the Superior the most respectable and holy of men. He would, seemingly, not only receive me with pleasure but would also offer me help should I be in a case of needing it.

'He is called the Reverend Father Raphael,' she continued; 'he is an Italian but has spent his life in France. He prefers to live in this solitude and has refused from the Pope – to whom he is related – the offer of several excellent benefices. He is a man of noble family, gentle, obliging, remarkably zealous and pious, and is about fifty years old. He is regarded by everyone in this part of the country as a saint.'

My interest was inflamed yet more by this recital. So much so that I could not resist the longing and the desire I felt to visit this holy church and by some pious acts repair therein those sins of which I had been guilty. When I reached the plain I could no longer see the belfry; I had only the forest to guide me and my sole route was a little trodden path which I was obliged to follow at random. When the sun had sunk below the horizon so that it no longer brightened the universe, I seemed to hear the distant sound of a bell. I stopped and listened, and then advanced in the direction of the noise. I began to hasten, and noticed that the path was becoming wider. Shortly I reached an opening and in front of me saw some hedges with, beyond them, the convent. No other dwellings stood near it – the closest were six leagues distant – and immense woods surrounded it on every side. Such was the convent of Sainte-Marie-des-Bois, and as it was situated in a hollow I had continually to descend in order to reach it – which was why it had been impossible for me to see the belfry from the plain. The hut of a gardening brother was built against the wall of the inner part of the building, and it was here that one requested entry. I ask this holy man if I might be permitted to speak to the Superior . . . He asked me what I might require of him . . . I replied that my religious duty – that a vow – had drawn me to this saintly retreat and that I would be well rewarded for all the pain it had cost me to come here if, for a moment, I could throw myself at the feet of the Virgin, and at those of the holy director in whose house this miraculous image dwelt.

Having asked me to rest, this brother speedily entered the convent. But, as it was already night and the fathers were at supper, it was some time before he returned. When he reappeared he was accompanied by another monk: 'This is father Clément, Mademoiselle,' he said to me, 'he is steward to our house, and has come to find out if what you require is important enough for him to disturb the Superior.'

Father Clément was a man of forty-five, enormously bulky and gigantic in build. He was surly and grim with a harsh, rough voice, and even at this first meeting it made me tremble much more than it reassured me . . . An involuntary shuddering immediately seized me; and, without my being able to do anything about it, the memory of all my past sufferings surged up in my memory.

'What do you want?' he asked me unfeelingly. 'Is this the sort of hour to come to a church? You look to me very much like an adventuress!'

'Holy man,' I said, prostrating myself before him, 'I have always believed that any time was a fit one to enter the house of God. I have travelled far to get here, fervour and devotion being my support, and I beg to confess, if it is possible. When my conscience shall be known to you it will be possible for you to judge whether or not I am worthy to prostrate myself at the feet of the miraculous image which is preserved within this holy house.'

'But this is scarcely the hour for confession,' said the monk, as he softened. 'Where will you pass the night? We have nowhere for you to stay, and it would be better for you to return in the morning.'

At this I explained how I had been hindered, and without replying further he went to give an account of me to the Superior. Several minutes later I heard the church door open and the Superior himself came towards the hut, inviting me to enter the main building with him. Father Raphael, of whom it seems best to give you a description immediately, was a man whose age I had been told, but to whom nobody would have ascribed even forty years. He was slender and reasonably tall with a sweet and intellectual face. He spoke French very well but with a slight Italian accent. In exteriors he presented polished manners and an obliging nature, but inwardly he was wild and sullen – as I shall have only too many occasions of convincing you.

'My child,' he said to me, in a gracious and gentle voice, 'although the hour is unreasonable and we are not in the habit of receiving so late I shall, nevertheless, hear your confession and afterwards we shall think of some means for enabling you to pass the night until the hour, tomorrow, when you may kneel before our holy image.'

Having said this, the monk lit several lamps around the confessional. He told me to place myself therein, and having sent away his companion and closed all the doors, he asked me to confide everything to him in the fullest assurance of his understanding. Perfectly at ease in front of such a considerate man, and disburdened of the terror which Father Clément had roused in me, I knelt submissively at his feet and opened myself entirely to him with all my usual candour and trust. I admitted each of my faults and related every misfortune, one after the other. Nothing was omitted – not even the shameful mark with which the execrable Rodin had stigmatised me.

Father Raphael listened with the greatest attention, even making me repeat certain details as he expressed his pity and concern . . . His principal questions were repeatedly directed toward the following subjects:

1. If it was really true that I was an orphan and came from Paris.

2. If I was quite sure that I had neither friends nor relatives, patrons, nor any other person to whom I might write.

3. Whether it was true that I had told only the shepherdess of my intention to visit the monastery and if I had arranged to meet her again on my return journey.

4. If it was true that I was really a virgin, and no older than twenty-two.

5. If I was absolutely certain that I had not been followed by anyone, and that nobody had seen me enter the monastery.

I was able completely to satisfy him on these points, and answered with all the innocence in the world.

'Very well, then,' said the monk, as he got up and took me by the hand; 'come along, my child. It is too late for you to kneel before the Virgin tonight. But tomorrow I shall arrange for you the sweet satisfaction of receiving communion at the feet of her image. In the meantime let us think about your bedroom, and what we are going to give you for supper.'

As he said this he led me towards the sacristy.

'What did you say?' I exclaimed, with a sensation of misgiving over which I had no control. 'Do you mean to say, Father, that you are taking me to the interior part of your house?'

'And where else, my charming pilgrim?' rejoined the monk as he opened a door off the cloister which led into the sacristy, thus bringing us right into the central portion of the house.

'Don't tell me you are afraid of spending the night with four monks! Ah! But you will see that we aren't the bigots we are supposed to be, for we know how to amuse ourselves with a pretty girl . . .'

These words startled me: 'Oh, merciful heaven,' I said to myself, 'am I once more to become the victim of my feeling for goodness, of my need to approach religion through its most respected channel? Will these desires once again be punished as though they are crimes?' Meanwhile we advanced through the darkness, but nothing revealed our exact locality in the building or offered any pathway of escape.

The monk, who made me walk in front of him, noticed something of my resistance: 'Get along with you, you two-faced bitch,' he exclaimed with passionate anger, immediately changing his coaxing tone to one of the most studied insolence. 'Do you think there's time to draw back? Ye gods, you will soon begin to realise that you'd have been happier in a den of thieves rather than falling into the midst of a group of four Recollets.'

Causes for terror began to multiply so rapidly before my eyes that I had little time to be alarmed by these words. Hardly had they been uttered than the most alarming sight met my eyes. The door in front of us opened, and I saw around a table three monks and three young girls, all in the most indecent state in the world. Two of these girls were completely naked, while the third was being undressed. As for the monks, they were more or less in the same state. . . .

'My friends,' said Raphael, as he entered: 'we were in need of an extra girl, and here she is. Allow me to present you with a true phenomenon. Here is a Lucrecia who actually bears on her shoulder the mark of girls of ill-fame. And there,' he continued, with a gesture as significant as it was indecent, 'there is the proof of an acknowledged virginity.'

Shrieks of laughter echoed from every corner of the room at this singular introduction; and Clément, whom I had met on my arrival and who was already somewhat drunk, immediately cried that such facts must instantly be verified. The necessity of describing these people to you obliges me to interrupt my narrative at this point. But I will keep you in suspense as to my situation for the shortest while possible.

Your acquaintance with Raphael and Clément is sufficient to allow me to pass on to the others. Antonin, the third of the Fathers in this monastery, was a little man of forty, spare and gaunt with a fiery temperament, the face of a satyr, and as hairy as a bear. He was insanely depraved – experienced the greatest delight in tormenting people – and his wickedness was unequalled. Father Jérôme, the senior member of the house, was an old libertine of sixty, as hard and brutal as Clément and even more of a drunkard. Surfeited with ordinary pleasures he was obliged, in order to recapture the glow of voluptuous sensation, to have recourse to pursuits as depraved as they were disgusting.

Florette was the youngest of the girls. She came from Dijon and was about fourteen, being the daughter of a prominent citizen of that town. She had been abducted by satellites of Raphael, who was rich and commanded considerable influence in his order, and who neglected nothing which might serve his passions. She was a brunette with very pretty eyes and a great deal of piquancy in her expression. Cornelie was about sixteen. She was blond, and most interesting in manner, with the loveliest of hair, the smoothest of complexions, and the most attractive figure possible. The daughter of a wine merchant, she came from Auxerre and had been seduced by Raphael himself, who had secretly entangled her in his snares. Omphale was a woman of thirty, very tall, with the most pronounced curves, a fine bosom, superb hair, a sweet and agreeable face, and the tenderest eyes it would be possible to see. She was the daughter of a prosperous wine-grower of Joigny, and had been on the eve of her marriage to a very wealthy man when Jérôme, with the most extraordinary enticements, coaxed her away from her family. At that time she had been only sixteen. Such was the society with whom I was destined to live. Such, also, was the sewer of impurity and filth to which I had come, expecting only to find that virtue and chastity which usually resides in holy retreats.

I was made to understand that since I was now a member of this terrifying circle, the best I could do would be to imitate the submission of my companions.

'It takes little imagination,' said Raphael, 'to realise that any attempt at resistance would be quite useless in this inaccessible retreat – a retreat to which you have been led by your unlucky star! You say you have suffered many misfortunes – which, according to your story, seems true. But if you examine the list of your misfortunes, you will see that the greatest piece of ill-luck a girl can suffer is still missing from it. Is it natural to remain virgin at your age? Isn't it a species of miracle which cannot be allowed to persist any longer? . . . Your companions here, like you, created a fuss when they found themselves obliged to serve us; and just as you are wisely going to do, they finished by submitting – when they saw that any other behaviour could bring them nothing but bad treatment.

'Finding yourself in the situation you are in, Sophie, how can you hope to defend yourself? Cast your thoughts over the way the world has abandoned you! On your own admission you have neither parents nor friends. See your situation as though you were in a desert, far from help, your whereabouts unknown to anyone on earth, and fallen into the hands of four libertines who assuredly have no desire to spare you . . . To whose assistance, then, will you have recourse? Will it be to that God whom you recently implored with so much zeal, and who profited by your fervour only to precipitate you the more surely into this trap.

'So you see, then, there is no power either human or divine which can snatch you from our hands. Nor is there anything in the realm of possibility – nor yet in the region of miracles – by means of which this virtue, of which you are so proud, can any longer be conserved. Nor is there anything which can prevent you from becoming, in every sense of the word and in every conceivable manner, the prey of the obscene excesses into which all four of us are going to plunge with you. Remove your clothes, then, Sophie, and may the most utter resignation earn you some kindness on our part. I warn you, however, that if you do not submit this will instantly be replaced by the most unfeeling and ignominious treatment – which will only provoke us further without in any way removing you from our intemperance and brutality.'

I knew only too well that this terrible discourse left me without resource; but would I not have been guilty had I not employed the means which my heart whispered, and which nature still left me? I threw myself at Raphael's feet, summoning all the forces of my soul as I begged him not to abuse my situation. My bitter tears flowed over his knees, and I dared to face him with the most moving arguments I could find. I did not yet know that tears become a further stimulant to the devotees of crime and debauchery. I was completely blind to the fact that my attempts to soften these monsters inflamed them only the more . . .

Then Raphael, furious, stood up: 'Take this vagabond, Antonin,' he exclaimed, frowning, '– take her and strip her this very instant! Teach her that compassion has no existence among men such as we!'

Antonin seized me with a lean but vigorous arm, and mingling his words and actions with frightful oaths, in two minutes he had torn off my clothes and presented me naked before the eyes of the assembly.

'There we have a beautiful creature!' said Jérôme. 'May this monastery fall and crush me if, in thirty years, I have seen a prettier!'

'Just a moment,' exclaimed the Superior; 'let us employ a little order in our proceedings. You are all aware, my friends, of our rules concerning reception. Let her be submitted to all of them, without exception; and during this time let the other three women remain beside us so as to anticipate our needs – or to excite them.'

A circle was formed and I was placed in the centre. There for more than two hours I was examined, considered and felt by these four libertines, exciting from each in turn either eulogy or criticism.

'You will allow me, Madame,' said our beautiful prisoner, blushing exceedingly, 'to conceal from you some of the obscene details observed at this first ceremony. Your imagination can supply you with all that debauchery could dictate in such circumstances to this group of lecherous men. You can picture them passing successively from my companions to myself, comparing, opposing, reconciling, and discussing various points. Even then you will have but the faintest idea of the kind of thing that happened during these first orgies – which were very mild in comparison with all the horrors of which I was shortly to become the victim.'

'Come,' said Raphael, whose prodigiously inflamed desires seemed to have reached the point at which it was no longer possible to restrain them, 'it is time to immolate the victim. Let each of us prepare to submit her to his favourite pleasure.'

And this coarsest of men, having placed me on a sofa in the attitude most propitious to his execrable pleasures, had me held down by Antonin and Clément ... Raphael, the depraved Italian monk, satisfied himself outrageously – without my ceasing to be a virgin. Oh, most awful of aberrations! It seemed that each of these crapulous men felt his glory to lie in leaving nature outside his choice when indulging his infamous pleasures ...

Clément was the next to approach me. Already inflamed by his Superior's behaviour, he was even more excited by the things he had done while observing this. He declared that he would represent no more danger for me than his confrère had done, and that the place where his homage was to be uttered would leave me without peril to my virtue. He made me get down on my knees, and fastening himself to me while in this position exercised his perfidious passions on me in a place which prevented me, during the sacrifice, from expressing any complaint as to its irregularity.

Jérôme followed. His temple was the same as that of Raphael, but he did not approach the sanctuary. Content to remain in the courtyard, and moved by primitive episodes the obscenity of which it is impossible to describe, he was unable to accomplish his desires except by the barbarous means of which I almost became a victim in the house of Dubourg and of which I was completely so in the hands of de Bressac.

'What favourable preparations,' exclaimed Antonin, as he seized hold of me. 'Come along, my little chicken, come along and let me avenge you for the irregularity of my confrères. Let me gather, at last, the delightful fruits abandoned to me by their intemperance!'

But the details! ... Great God! ... I cannot possibly describe them to you. One might have said that this flagitious villain – who was the most lecherous of the four, even though he appeared the least removed from nature's ways – only consented to approach me with a little less inconformity providing he could compensate himself for this lesser depravity by outraging me more thoroughly, and for a longer period ... Alas, if at times I had previously allowed my imagination to wander over the pleasures of sex, I believed them chaste as the God who inspires them, given by nature as a consolation to human beings and born of love and tenderness. I had been far from believing that man, following the example of certain ferocious beasts, was able to enjoy himself only by making his partners shriek with pain. My experience was so violent that the sufferings natural to the breaking of my virginity were the least I had to support in this dangerous attack. But it was at the moment of his crisis, which Antonin terminated with such furious cries, with such murderous excursions over every part of my body, and bitings so like the bloody caresses of a tiger, that I felt for a moment I was the prey of some savage animal who could only be appeased by devouring me. Once these horrors had ceased I fell back on the altar of my immolation, motionless and almost unconscious.

Raphael ordered the women to look after me and give me something to eat. But in that cruel moment a raging torrent of grief and desolation was sweeping through my heart. I had finally lost the treasure of my virginity – for which I would have sacrificed my life a hundred times. Nor could I accept the fact that I had been dishonoured by those from whom I had expected the greatest assistance and moral support. My tears flowed abundantly, my cries echoed round the room. I rolled on the floor, tore my hair, and begged my butchers to put me to death. But although these profligate wretches had become completely hardened to such scenes and were far more interested in tasting of new pleasures with my companions than in calming my pain or comforting me, they were nevertheless sufficiently troubled by my cries to send me off to rest in a place where my lamentations could not be heard . . . Omphale was ready to take me there when the perfidious Raphael, still looking at me with lubricity despite the cruel state I was in, said that he did not want me sent away before I had once more become his victim . . . Hardly had he conceived this project than it was executed . . . His desires, however, needed an additional degree of stimulation, and it was not until he had employed the cruel methods of Jérôme that he found the necessary strength for the accomplishment of this new crime . . . What excesses of debauchery! Great God! – was it possible that these lubricious beasts could be so ferocious as to choose the moment of crisis of a moral pain so violent as mine to make me suffer an equally barbarous physical one?

'By all that's merry,' exclaimed Antonin as he also took me again, 'it's good to follow the example of one's superior; and nothing is so appetising as a second offence. They tell me that pain inclines one to pleasure. I'm sure this beautiful child is going to make me the happiest of men!'

And despite my repugnance, despite all my cries and pleas, I became for a second time the wretched target of this contemptible satyr . . . At length they allowed me to go.

'If I had not already indulged before this lovely princess arrived,' said Clément, 'she would not be leaving this room before I had served my passions a second time – but she will lose nothing by waiting.'

'I promise her the same,' said Jérôme, making me feel the strength of his arm as I passed near him. 'But, so far as tonight is concerned, let us all go to bed.'

Raphael being of the same opinion, the orgies were interrupted. He kept Florette with him, and she doubtless stayed the night; but the remainder of the party returned to their rooms. I was looked after by Omphale. This sultana, older than the others, appeared to be in charge of the sisters. She took me to our apartment. It was situated in a kind of square tower in each corner of which was a bed. It was usual for one of the monks to follow the girls when they retired and to lock the door with two or three bolts. Clément was the brother who had been charged with this duty. Once inside, it was certainly impossible to get out, as there was no other exit from this room – apart from a small toilet, the window of which was as narrow and barred as that of the place in which we slept. There was little furniture – a chair and table stood by each bed, which was surrounded by printed curtains of the poorest quality. In addition there were some wooden chests in a cupboard, a few pierced chairs, some bidets, and a communal dressing-table. But it was not until the next day that I noticed all this. Too overcome to see anything during these first moments I could think of nothing but my pain.

'Oh, God, who decrees all,' I said to myself, 'is it therefore written that no virtuous act shall be suggested by my heart but it shall immediately be followed by misfortune? What evil have I done, oh most merciful Father, in wishing to perform in this house naught but pious duties? Have I offended heaven by this devotion? Is the treatment I have received the reward I should have expected? Oh incomprehensible decrees of providence, deign for an instant to guide my understanding if you wish to prevent me from revolting against your laws!' Bitter tears followed these reflections; and I was still immersed in them when Dom Clément arrived, as heated with wine as he was with lust and followed by a girl of twenty-six named Armande, who was to join in the proposed affair . . . The filthy monk did everything, even to gnawing the tongue and lips of the poor girl, while I was forced to whip him slightly the while. Then he drove us through such orgies of pain that we could hardly sustain them.

'Let us lie down,' he finally said to me; 'perhaps you have suffered too much, my dear, even though not enough for me . . . Ah! dear girl, you have no idea how far this depravity drags us – the intoxication into which it throws us, the violent commotions which result in our nervous fluid from the irritation produced by the pain of the object who serves our passions. How one is tickled by one's evils! The desire of increasing our pleasures! – that's the stumbling block of this fantasy, and I know it! Yet should such a thing be feared by a man who mocks everything? . . .

I attempted to reproach him with the degeneracy manifested in his tastes; but the manner in which this libertine justified them seems to me to deserve some space in the history of what befell me.

'The most ridiculous thing in the world, my dear, is doubtless the wish to dispute a man's tastes – to attempt to thwart them, blame them, punish them – should they not be in conformity, either with the accepted laws of the country we happen to inhabit, or with social conventions. What men will never understand is that there is no kind of taste or preference, however odd, however criminal one might suppose it to be, but depends on the kind of individual organisation we have received from nature. This being so, what right, I ask, has one man to dare to require of another man either that he reform his tastes or attempt to model them after that of the social order? Moreover, what right have the laws, which are merely formulated for man's happiness, what right have these laws to punish the man who is not able to correct himself strictly according to their codes? – or who would succeed in doing so only at the expense of that happiness which the laws should conserve for him? . . .

'Let us go into a few particulars . . . You are astonished at the poignant feelings and sensations felt by some of our fellows for things usually known as disgusting or degrading, and you are likewise surprised because our voluptuous faculties are profoundly moved by actions which, according to your own judgement, bear only the stamp and emblem of ferocity. Let us analyse these tastes . . .

'It is strange, you pretend, that dirty and intemperate things can produce in our senses that irritation essential for the completion of such delirium; but far from being astonished at this you should understand, my dear, that objects have no value in our eyes except that which our imagination sets on them; it is, therefore, quite possible, according to this constant truth, that not only the oddest things but also the most vile and most shocking may affect us very sensibly . . .

'Such is man's imagination that the same object presents itself to different men under as many shapes as it has different modes. And according to the effect, whatever it may be, resulting from our interpretation of the object, the imagination becomes determined to love it – or to hate it. According to this reasoning it is not at all surprising that what greatly delights some may equally displease others; and vice versa, that the most extraordinary things may find sectarians . . . As is well known, the ugly man is able to find mirrors wherein he looks handsome.

'Now, if we grant that the enjoyment of the senses is always dependent on the imagination, we should no longer be astonished at the numerous variations which imagination will suggest in these enjoyments – at the host of tastes and different passions which the wanderings of imagination will produce. Three quarters of the population of the world may find the smell of a rose delicious without it serving as any proof either to condemn the quarter who might find such a perfume actually unpleasant, or to show that this smell is truly agreeable.

'If there exist, therefore, in the world, beings whose tastes are in opposition to the admitted prejudices, not only must we refuse to be astonished at them, not only must we avoid finding fault with them and refrain from punishing them – but we must render them some service, try to content them, destroy the curbs and restrictions which vex them, and afford them – if you will be just – every means of satisfying themselves without risk. For they are no more responsible for their strange tastes than you are for being witty or stupid, well-formed or hump-backed. The organs which make us susceptible to such-and-such a fantasy are formed in our mother's womb; the first sights presented to our infantile eyes, the first discourses we ever hear, all these ultimately combine to determine our actions and reactions – our tastes are formed thus, and nothing in the world can henceforth destroy them.

'It is in vain that education sets to work: it never really alters anything, and he who is born a villain becomes one however sound the education he receives. And just as surely, the man whose organs function towards goodness hastens equally as quickly in the pathway of virtue, even though he lack both a teacher and a model. Both have acted according to their physical organisation, according to the impressions they have received from nature, and the one is not more deserving of punishment than the other of reward.

'What strikes me as most surprising is that when it is simply a question of trivial things we are never astonished at the difference in tastes between one individual and another; but the moment these differences involve what is known as lust – behold, everything is in an uproar! Yet what an injustice! As I said previously, the man with strange tastes is a sick man, and it is just as silly and cruel to punish such a man, whatever his faults and errors, as it is to punish, mock, or ridicule a man who is crippled. Wouldn't he be normal if he had it in him! – who wouldn't? But when anatomy and physiology are really perfected, it will be clearly demonstrated that all morality is essentially physical. What will become then of your laws, ethics, religion, gibbets, paradise, God, and hell – when it is proved that a particular organisation of the nerves, a peculiar reaction in the body, a certain degree of acridity in the blood, makes a man what he is, for better or for worse? You say our cruelty amazes you? Why? What is the object of the man who seeks sensual pleasure? Is it not to allow his senses all the stimulus they are capable of experiencing? And this in order that he may arrive at his final paroxysms more successfully and speedy? The supreme pleasure – that is the thing! And it is more or less enjoyable according to the type of activity chosen. For his pleasure to be increased it is not at all necessary that it be shared by the woman. In fact is it not evident that every pleasure the woman shares with us, she takes away from us? And why is it necessary that she should experience pleasure at the same time as ourselves? It is surely more pleasing that she should not do so, so that we may enjoy ourselves unhampered, with nothing to hinder us from concentrating solely on our own pleasures. This flatters our pride the more. Not delicate, I admit; yet why should delicacy enter into these matters? Consideration of it represents an obnoxious attitude in relation to pleasure. Delicacy, for instance, may go hand in hand with love and romance; but love and sexual pleasure are not necessarily the same thing – they frequently, in fact, represent two entirely different attitudes. People daily love each other without enjoying, and enjoy each other without loving. And whatever is related to delicacy is to the advantage of the woman at the expense of that of the man . . . Thus, if selfishness is the primal law of nature, how equally true it is that it must occupy this same position in the pleasures of the passions!

'Moreover, if you consider what I have just said, you will realise that isolated ecstasies also possess charms – may even present more of them than any other pleasures. If it were not so, how would so many old men, so many ugly people and defective folk, find pleasure? They know quite well that they are not loved; they are absolutely certain that it is impossible for any partner to share their feelings – yet do they experience any the less voluptuous sensation on that account? Do they merely desire an illusion? . . . It is, therefore, not at all necessary to bestow pleasure in order to receive it. Thus the happy or the unhappy situation of the victims of our debauchery becomes a matter of unconcern for us and does not affect the satisfaction of our senses one jot! . . . Is any reasonable man truly anxious to have his pleasure shared by a loose woman? And are there not millions of men who find great delight with these creatures? If this, then, is true, there must be countless individuals persuaded of the law I establish, who practise it without suspecting it – and who, at the same time, foolishly blame others who would justify their actions by sound principles.

'If nature was offended by various tastes she would avoid planting them in our breasts. It is impossible that we should receive from her any sentiment which might outrage her; and resting in this absolute certainty, we should give rein to our passions, whatsoever they be, for we may be sure that any drawbacks they may entail are mere designs of nature whose unwilling pawns we are . . . '

When Clément had ceased talking I asked him if they kept the poor girls for ever in the convent, miserable and unhappy – 'Surely you send them away when you have tired of them?' I added.

'Yes, yes . . . ' he replied. 'When we have decided to grant you a retreat you shall have it most certainly . . . '

I learned later what this meant.

As dawn began to break, Omphale approached my bed.

'My dear friend,' she said, 'I come to exhort you to take courage. During my first days here I wept just as you have done. But habit has accustomed me to this life, and it will be likewise with you. The first moments are terrible, I know . . . Not only because we are perpetually obliged to gratify the unbounded passions of these debauches – which, in itself, is torture enough – but also because of the loss of our freedom and the brutal way in which we are treated in this infamous house . . . Nevertheless, unhappy as we are, we derive some comfort from seeing others suffering in the same manner as ourselves.'

My pain was still unbearable, yet I managed to conquer it for a moment that I might beg my companion to acquaint me with whatever further evils I might expect.

'Listen,' said Omphale, as she seated herself near my bed, 'I am going to speak to you in all confidence – but remember, you must never abuse it . . . The cruellest of our sufferings, dear friend, is the uncertainty of our fate – for it is quite impossible to say what becomes of us when we leave this place. We have as much proof as our isolation permits us to gather that none of the girls discharged by the monks has ever reappeared in the outside world. In fact they have themselves hinted at it, for they don't hide from us the knowledge that this retreat is also our tomb. Every year two or three girls leave us. And what becomes of them? Are they done away with? To this question the monks sometimes answer yes; at others they reply with an emphatic no! But of those who have left this place none, whatever promises they may have made that they would lodge complaints about this monastery in the right quarters and work for our liberation – none, I repeat, has ever kept her word. Are the brothers able satisfactorily to account for these complaints, or do they completely prevent these girls from being able to make them? When we ask newcomers for news of former girls they only reply that they know nothing about them.

'What becomes of these unfortunate creatures? That is what torments us, Sophie – and it is this terrible uncertainty that tortures our unhappy days. It is fourteen years since I was first brought to this place, and in that period I have seen more than fifty girls disappear from here . . . Where are they? How is it that, of all those who have sworn to help us, not one has been able to keep her word? The number of girls kept here is always fixed at four – at least so far as this room is concerned. But we are all more than persuaded that there is another tower corresponding to this one where they keep an equal number of prisoners. Many things in the conduct of these wretches – as well as bits of their conversation – have convinced us of this. But if we do have such comrades here we have never seen them. One of the strongest proofs we have supporting this belief is that we never serve them two days running. Yesterday we were employed; today we shall take it easy. But it seems impossible that these debauchees could abstain for a day! Moreover, they have no specific rule regarding our dismissal from service – it has nothing to do with age, diminishing beauty, boredom, or disgust – nothing but their caprice is the determining factor in these decisions to grant us a sinister leave of absence – regarding which we have no means of knowing whether we shall fare well or ill.

'We had here a woman of seventy who left only last summer. She had been here sixty years, and during the time of her residence I have seen the discharge of more than twelve girls under sixteen. Some have vanished three days after their arrival, others at the end of a month, and yet others only after many years. There is no rule about it whatever other than what is dictated by their whim. And our behaviour is equally unimportant. I have seen girls who could more than cope with the desires of these men, and yet they were dismissed after only six weeks. On the other hand there have been sulky and capricious creatures whom they have kept for many years. It is thus useless to attempt to formulate any kind of law regarding behaviour for the benefit of new arrivals. Their unpredictability overthrows every law. Nothing is certain with them.

'As for the monks themselves, they rarely change. It is fifteen years since Raphael came here; Clément has been with us sixteen, Jérôme thirty, and Antonin ten. He is the only one I have actually seen arriving, and he came to replace a sixty-year-old monk who died during an excess of debauchery. Raphael, a Florentine by birth, is a near relative of the Pope, with whom he stands in great favour. It is only since his arrival that the miraculous Virgin has assured the reputation of the monastery by hindering those of a scandalous turn of mind from noticing too much of what goes on here. But otherwise everything here was just as it is when he first joined us. It has been like this for almost eighty years, so I'm told; and every new Superior has automatically preserved an arrangement so advantageous for his pleasure. Raphael, who is reputed to be one of the most licentious monks of the present century, sought an appointment here only because he knew what went on, and it is his intention to preserve for as long as ever possible those secret privileges of which you are aware. We are situated in the diocese of Auxerre; but, whether or not the Bishop has been informed of the circumstances, we have never seen him make an appearance in this establishment. In fact few people frequent it – except during the time of the religious feast towards the end of August. Otherwise scarcely ten people visit the church in a year. When, however, strangers do present themselves the Superior is careful to receive them properly – and to impose on them with endless manifestations of austerity and religious sentiment. And so they go away pleased, praising the house. Thus the impunity of these vile criminals is bolstered by the good faith of the people and the credulity of the devout.

'As for the rest, nothing is so severe as the rules governing our behaviour – and nothing so dangerous as infringing them in any manner. In fact it is essential that I go into some details concerning this matter,' continued my instructress, 'for it is not accepted here as an excuse if you say: *Do not punish me for the infraction of this law, because I did not know about it.* The position is such that, if you don't learn about these rules from your companions, you must guess them yourself. You are given no warning as to anything and yet you are punished for everything. And the only form of correction permitted is the whip. It is thus easy enough for any of our faults to become an occasion for the favourite pleasure of these profligates. You suffered yesterday without breaking any of the laws – soon you will experience the same punishment for having erred. All four of them are infected by this barbarous mania, and each takes his turn at wielding the lash. Every day one of them is elected Regent of the Day, and receives a report from the room-mistress. He is also charged with ordering interior affairs and with the organisation of all that happens at those suppers to which we are bidden as compulsory guests. It is he who taxes us with our faults and he who punishes them.

'But let us consider our rules and customs in some detail: We are always obliged to be up and dressed by nine o'clock in the morning. At ten bread and water is brought to us for our breakfast. At two we are served with dinner, which consists of quite a good soup, a little stewed meat, some vegetables, and generally some fruit, together with a bottle of wine for all four of us. Regularly each day, come winter, come summer, the Regent visits us at five in the evening. That is when he receives his information from the room-mistress, and she is required to make a full report regarding the conduct of the girls in her room. She must give information concerning any signs of revolt, as to whether everyone rose when they should, whether all rules as to dress and cleanliness have been observed, if everyone has eaten as they should and whether any attempts at escape have been considered. Furthermore, she is herself punished should she fail to give a precise account of these things.

'After this the Regent examines various things. Once his business is completed it is rare that he should leave before he has amused himself with one of us – and often with all four. After he has left, should it not be our day for attending at supper, we are free to talk, read, and relax together and to go to bed when we wish. If we are to sup with the monks that evening a bell rings to warn us to prepare ourselves. The Regent himself comes to seek us and we descend into that room where you first saw us naked. Once there, the first thing they do is to read the record of our faults committed since our previous visit. First, those committed at the preceding supper – which comprise: negligence, frigidity towards the monks, inattentiveness, and uncleanliness. To these is added the list of faults committed in our room during the two-day interval between orgies. One after the other the delinquents place themselves in the centre of the room, and the Regent of the day names their faults and punishment. They are then stripped naked by the room-mistress – or by her immediate inferior should she herself be guilty of offence. Then the Regent administers the prescribed chastisement, and so energetically that it is difficult to forget it. But the craftiness of these rogues is so considerable that there is scarcely a meeting but several such floggings take place.

'This business completed, the orgies commence. To give you an idea of their range would be impossible. The bizarre caprices of the brothers are without precedent, and the essential thing, while never refusing them anything, is to anticipate everything . . . Yet, advisable as this course is, one can never be sure of approval. About halfway through the orgies they have their meal. We are allowed to partake of this, and it is always much more sumptuous and delicate than our own fare. The bacchanal really commences when the monks are half drunk. At midnight the party breaks up and each monk has the right to keep one of us with him throughout the hours of darkness. This favourite sleeps with whoever has chosen her, returning to her companions next morning. The remainder return to their room, finding it clean and the beds and wardrobes in perfect order. Sometimes, before the hour of breakfast, one of the brothers may send and request a girl to visit him in his cell. The one who is charged with our welfare comes to seek us and conducts us to the monk who has asked for us – who then brings us back himself, or returns us in the care of this same brother once he has no further need for us.

'This cerberus who cleans our room and sometimes conducts us is an old monk whom you will soon see. He is seventy, has only one eye, and is lame and mute. There are three others who assist him in his duties. One prepares and cooks the food; another looks after the Fathers' cells, sweeps, and also helps in the kitchen; and, finally, there is the porter you saw when you arrived. We never see any of these men excepting the one who serves us, and the slightest word to him would constitute the gravest of offences. Sometimes the Superior visits us . . . Finally there are certain customary ceremonies which experience will teach you, but the non-observance of which is a crime. And each day our masters' appetite for the pleasures of punishment stimulates them to multiply the number of possible offences. Raphael rarely visits us unless he has some project in view, and these – as you have already had occasion to realise – are either cruel or irregular. For the rest, we are always carefully confined within these walls, never being allowed outside even to take the air. For, although there is a large enough garden, it is not fitted with bars, and our captors are too afraid we might escape by that route. Such, of course, would be most dangerous for them; since information received either by the temporal or spiritual authorities disclosing all the crimes committed here would soon result in everything being set to order. As to religion, we never fulfil any duties in that direction and it is as much forbidden us to think of it as to speak of it. This, I feel, is one of the griefs inflicted on us most deserving of punishment.

'And that, my dear companion, is all I can tell you,' said our room-mistress. 'Experience,' she added, 'will teach you the rest. Be courageous, if you can; but give up every thought of the outside world. There is no instance of any girl dismissed from here ever having seen it again.'

Disturbed extremely by this last remark, I asked Omphale what she really thought about the fate of the discharged girls.

'What can I say about that?' she remarked. 'Whilst hope may bid us believe otherwise, everything seems to prove to me that only a grave can be our gateway to escape . . .

'We are informed on the morning of the day that a discharge has been arranged,' continued Omphale. 'The Regent for that day visits us before breakfast and says something like this: *Omphale, pack your bag, for you are discharged from the monastery. I shall come back for you this evening.* Then he leaves us. The girl who has received her discharge embraces her companions and promises them a thousand thousand times that she will help them, complain in the right quarters, and make a considerable noise about all that goes on. The hour strikes, the monk comes, the girl leaves, and is never heard of again. Nevertheless, if it happens to be one of the days for supper, the party takes place as usual. The only difference we have noticed during such orgies is that the monks indulge much less in their pleasures, drink far more, send us away much earlier, and never go to bed with any of us.'

'My dear friend,' I said to the room-mistress as I thanked her for this information, 'surely these girls must have been children who lacked the strength of character to keep their word? But let us make a mutual promise! For my own part I swear to you in advance, and by all that I hold most sacred, I shall either die or I shall destroy these infamies. Will you promise me as much yourself?'

'Certainly,' said Omphale; 'but you may rest assured that these promises are absolutely useless. For girls older than you, girls perhaps even more infuriated than you are – if such is possible – and these belonging to the influential families of the district – being armed, therefore, with more efficient weapons than yourself – girls, in a word, who would have given their very life's blood for me, have all failed in keeping these same vows. Let me, therefore, with my cruel experience, regard the present one as equally vain and no more to be relied on.'

After this we chatted for a while about the characters of the monks and those of our companions.

'There are no more dangerous men in Europe,' Omphale continued, 'than Raphael and Antonin. Duplicity, blackness of heart, wickedness, torture, cruelty, and irreligion are their natural qualities, and joy never lightens their eyes save when they give themselves unreservedly to their vices.

'Clément, who appears more brusque, is really the best of them and is only to be feared when he is drunk – but at such times one must be very careful to keep out of his way, for then there is considerable risk for anyone who happens to meet him. As for Jérôme, he is naturally brutal. Slaps, kicks and punches are the certain income of those who are with him, but once his passions have been satisfied he becomes gentle as a lamb. Such is the essential difference between him and the first two, who can only reanimate their desires by way of treachery and atrocity.

'So far as the girls are concerned,' she continued, 'there is little to be said. Florette is not a very intelligent child, and one can do with her just as one wishes. Cornélie is much more spiritual and sensitive, and nothing can console her for the fate which has befallen her.'

After receiving this information, I asked my companion if it was really quite impossible to discover whether or not there was another tower containing other unfortunates such as ourselves.

'If they exist – and I am almost certain of it,' said Omphale, ' it could only be ascertained through some indiscretion of the monks or from the mute brother who serves us and doubtless looks after them as well. But such an attempt would be extremely dangerous. Besides, what point would be served by finding out whether or not we are alone here, for whatever may be the case we should not be able to help ourselves. If you nevertheless insist on demanding whether I have any proof that this likelihood is more than probable, I can tell you that many of the careless remarks of the brothers are more than sufficient to convince us. Besides, one morning after I had been sleeping with Raphael, as I crossed his threshold and he followed so as to lead me back to our room, without his noticing anything I saw the mute entering Antonin's cell accompanied by a very beautiful girl of seventeen or eighteen – who certainly did not belong to our group. The monk, realising that he had been seen, quickly pushed her into the cell – but not before I had realised what was happening. He did not register any complaint and the matter rested there. So it is certain that there are other women here, and that as we sup with the monks only on alternate days, they must sup with them in the intervals – probably in similar numbers.'

Scarcely had Omphale finished speaking than Florette returned from Raphael's cell where she had spent the night. And, as it was absolutely forbidden for the girls to tell each other what happened to them on such occasions, seeing us awake she simply wished us good-morning and threw herself, exhausted, on her bed – where she remained until nine, the general hour of rising. It was then that the tender Cornélie came to me, weeping as she looked at me . . . and she said: 'Oh, my dear young friend, what unfortunate creatures we are!'

Breakfast was brought in. My companions forced me to eat a little, and I complied so as to please. The remainder of the day passed quietly enough; but at five, as Omphale had explained, the Regent entered.

It was Antonin and he laughingly enquired how I felt after my adventure. When, however, I replied only by lowering my eyes – which were still flooded with tears – he sneered, and said: 'She'll get used to it, she'll get used to it. There isn't a single house in France where they train girls better than we do.'

He continued on his round and took the list of faults handed him by the room-mistress – who was too kind-hearted to overburden it with details, frequently saying that she had nothing to report. Before leaving he approached me . . . I trembled, believing myself about to become, once more, the victim of this monster. A silly reaction; for since this was likely to happen at any moment, what did it matter whether it was now or the next day? I nevertheless escaped with only a few brutal caresses. But he threw himself upon Cornélie, ordering every one of us – while he performed – to assist him in his passions. The lecherous scoundrel gorged himself with voluptuous sensations of every type, denying himself nothing, and brought his encounter with this unfortunate girl to precisely the same kind of termination as he had indulged with me on the previous night. That is to say with the most deliberate acts of brutality and depravity.

This species of group activity took place very frequently. It was nearly always customary, when a monk was enjoying himself with one of the sisters, for the other three to surround him, exciting his senses in every part so that voluptuous ecstasy might diffuse itself throughout his entire being. I hint here at these impure details with the intention of not returning to them again, for I have no wish to dwell further on the indecency of these scenes. To paint one would be to paint all; and so far as my long residence in this house is concerned, I intend only to describe the essential events without horrifying you with further details. As the day I am speaking of did not happen to be our day for supper we were all peaceful enough. My companions did their best to comfort me, but nothing could soften the grief felt by one so sensitive as myself. They tried in vain, for the more they spoke of the evil which had befallen me the more did I feel the sharpness of its pain.

Next morning at nine the Superior came to see me, although it was not actually his day. He asked Omphale if I had begun to settle down and, without really listening to her reply, opened one of the chests in our cupboard, bringing out a number of female garments.

'As you brought nothing with you,' he said, 'we must think about clothing you – even if it is more for our own pleasure than for your comfort . . . And no gratitude, please! Personally I am not at all in favour of this useless apparel, and it wouldn't trouble me a bit if we allowed the girls who serve us to remain as naked as animals. But our Fathers are men of the world, men who wish for the luxury and elegance of raiment. And so they must be satisfied.'

And he threw on the bed several dressing-gowns, half a dozen chemises, a few caps, some stockings, and some slippers. He told me to try them on and assisted me in my dressing so as to touch me as indecently as the situation permitted. Three taffeta gowns and one of Indian linen were found to fit me. He allowed me to keep them, and said that I could alter the remainder, remembering that they were all the property of the house and were to be returned should I leave. These details having procured him a few glimpses, which heated him, he ordered me to place myself in the position which I knew he preferred . . . I would have begged his mercy, but seeing the wrath of passion already in his eyes I realised that it would be more expedient to obey. So I took up my posture . . . The libertine, surrounded by the other three girls, satisfied himself as was his wont – at the expense of morals, of religion, and of nature. He was excited by me, and entertained me well at supper. I was, moreover, destined to spend the night with him. My companions retired, and I accompanied him to his apartment.

I will no longer speak to you, Madame, either of the revulsion I experienced, or the pain. You will doubtless be able to imagine how extreme they were; but the monotony of such descriptions, if repeated, would perhaps prejudice you against such further revelations as I must make. Raphael's cell was charming and furnished by a voluptuary who also had taste. It lacked nothing which might render his solitude agreeable, or his pleasures delightful. Once the door had been shut he stripped himself naked, ordering me to do likewise. Then for a long time I was obliged to excite his pleasure by the same method he later actively employed on me. I can say here that during the course of that evening I received so complete a tuition in lecherous exercise that my knowledge became equal to that of the most expert female practitioners of these impurities. Becoming a mistress in one art, however, it was essential that I should soon revert to the position of scholar – so as to learn another. And so the night progressed. . . . Raphael never for a moment asked indulgence of me, but I was soon in such a state that I was obliged, hot tears pouring from my eyes, to beg it of him. Yet he mocked at my pleas and took the most barbarous precautions against my attempts at movement. Then, when he saw himself master of the situation, he treated me – throughout two entire hours – with the most unexampled severity. Nor did he confine himself to those parts normally destined for such attack, but roamed indiscriminately over the most contrary places, the most delicate globes. Nothing escaped the fury of this butcher whose voluptuous titillations derived their intensity from his gloating observation of my pain.

'Let us go to bed,' he said, as he ceased his efforts. 'Perhaps this has been too much for you – although it certainly hasn't been enough for me! One never becomes exhausted by this divine exercise. All that I have done is but a semblance of what I should like to do!'

And so we went to bed. There, wanton and depraved as ever, Raphael made me throughout the night the slave of his criminal pleasures. During a moment of calm I seized the opportunity to beg his information as to whether I might hope, one day, to be released from this house.

'Most assuredly,' answered Raphael; 'you only came here so as to be able to leave us. When all four of us agree to grant your discharge you shall certainly have it.'

'But,' I said, hoping to elicit something more from him, 'aren't you afraid that girls younger than myself – and less discreet than I swear I shall be throughout my life – aren't you afraid one of them may reveal just what goes on here?'

'That is impossible,' exclaimed the Superior.

'Impossible?'

'Absolutely impossible, my girl!'

'Could you possibly explain this to me?'

'No! That is our secret. But I can certainly tell you that, discreet or not, it will be quite impossible for you ever to reveal any of our activities once you have left us.'

Having said this he brutally ordered me to change the subject, and I daren't say anything more. At seven in the morning I was led back to my room by the Brother who usually performed that office; and fitting together what I had learned from Raphael with what Omphale had told me, I was left with the dreadful certainty that the most violent means were employed against those girls who left the house. . . . If they never spoke to anyone it was for the simple reason that, shut up in their coffins, they weren't able to. I shuddered for a long time as I ruminated on this terrible idea, but finally managed to dispel it by combating it with hope. Like my companions, I was, in fact, benumbed.

Within a week I had made my circuit. During that period I became acquainted with all the deviations, all the diverse infamies which each of these monks indulged in turn – and that with the most terrifying rapidity . . . In every one of them the flame of lust was illumined only by an excess of ferocity. And this vice of corrupted hearts activated in them every other form of viciousness – for it was only by exercising such that they were able to crown their pleasures.

Antonin was the man who made me suffer most. It is impossible for anyone to imagine just how far this wicked wretch indulged his cruelty during the delirium of his aberrations. He was always stimulated by these mysterious tastes, which seemed to be the only ones conducive to his enjoyment. But they kept the flame burning brightly within him when he gave himself up to them, and they alone served to perfect it at its zenith. I was, nevertheless, astonished that his tastes were not instrumental – despite their rigour – in rendering some of his victims pregnant. So I asked our room-mistress how he managed to avoid such complications.

'By immediately, and personally, destroying the fruit resulting from his ardour,' said Omphale. 'As soon as he notices such a condition he makes us drink, for three days in succession, six large glasses of a special kind of tisane. And after four days no trace of his intemperance is left. It recently happened to Cornélie, and has happened to me three times. But it does not injure one's health. On the contrary we usually feel much better after it.'

'In any case,' she added, 'he is the only one – as you already know – from whom we need fear such complications. The irregularity of the desires of each of the others leaves us no room for doubt.'

Then Omphale asked me if I hadn't found Clément the least troublesome of the four.

'Alas,' I replied, 'amidst such a crowd of horrors and impurities, which alternately disgust and revolt me, it is difficult to say what wearies me least. Every one of them exhausts me, and already I wish to leave this place no matter what fate may hold in store.'

'It is possible that you may soon be satisfied,' said Omphale. 'It was by mere accident that you came here, and they had not relied on such a coincidence. Just eight days before your arrival they had discharged a girl, and they never proceed with such a course until they are certain of a replacement. Nor do they always find new recruits themselves. They have well-paid agents who serve them with fervour. So I feel almost certain that a new one is likely to arrive at any moment. Thus your wish may be gratified. Besides, we are on the eve of our religious festival. This is a time which rarely passes but it brings them something. They either seduce young girls at confession, or they kidnap them and lock them up. But it is rare that some young chicken isn't gobbled on such an occasion.

The celebrated feast day dawned at last. And you wouldn't believe, Madame, the monstrous impieties indulged by these monks during this event! Believing that a visible miracle would augment the brilliance of their reputation, they dressed Florette – the smallest and youngest of us – in all the ornaments and accoutrements of the Virgin; and attaching invisible cords to her waist ordered her to raise her arms towards heaven when the Host was lifted. The unfortunate little creature was menaced with the cruellest treatment if she uttered a single word, or in any way failed in her performance, with the result that she did her best, and the fraud enjoyed the greatest success one could possibly imagine. The people cried in one voice: 'Miracle! Miracle!' and left rich offerings for the Virgin – going away more convinced than ever of the efficacy and grace of this celestial mother.

Wishing to complete their impiety, our libertines decided that Florette should appear at supper in the same garments which had attracted so much reverence earlier in the day; and each of them inflamed his odious desires by submitting her to the irregularity of his caprice while she was thus clothed. Excited by this first crime, these monsters could not restrain themselves from going further. They stretched her naked, and on her belly, on a large table. Then, placing the image of our Saviour at her head and some lighted candles around her, they dared to consummate upon the loins of this unhappy creature the most fearful of our mysteries. This horrible spectacle was so unbearable that I fainted. When he saw this, Raphael said that in order to accustom me to such matters it was necessary that I should serve as altar in my turn. Seizing me, they placed me in the position which had been occupied by Florette, and the filthy Italian, punctuating his ritual with episodes even more atrocious and sacrilegious than before, consummated upon me the same fearful travesty as he had performed over my companion. When this was over I was no longer capable of movement. They had to carry me to my room where for three days I wept the bitterest of tears over the terrible crime in which I had been forced to participate. This memory still tears my very heart, Madame, and I never think of it without tears. Religion for me is a matter of feeling, and anything which offends or outrages my feelings makes my heart bleed.

Meanwhile, and so far as the new companion we were expecting was concerned, it did not seem that she had been chosen from amongst the crowd attracted by the religious festival. Such a girl may, of course, have been sent to the other seraglio; but nothing happened in ours. And everything continued in this way for a considerable time. I had already dwelt six weeks in this detestable house when Raphael entered our tower towards nine o'clock one morning. He seemed wild and excited, with a strange bewilderment in his glance. One after the other he examined us, placing each in the position he especially favoured. He stopped suddenly at Omphale, contemplating her for several long minutes as she maintained her posture. Moved by some secret agitation he gave himself up to one of his favourite practices, but without bringing it to consummation . . . Then, making her get up, he fixed her for a while with a severe glance, ferocity etching itself deep in his every feature.

'You have served us long enough,' he said at last. 'The society grants you your discharge, and I bring you our official permission to leave. Prepare yourself, for I shall come to seek you at nightfall.'

Having said this he examined her once again in the same old manner – and then abruptly left the room.

As soon as he was outside, Omphale threw herself into my arms.

'Ah!' she said, in tears. 'Here at last is the moment I have longed for, just as much as I fear it . . . What is going to happen to me, great God!'

I did all I could to calm her; but nothing was successful. She swore by the most sacred oaths that she would do everything in her power to deliver us, promising to lodge complaints against these traitors should they leave her the means. And her manner of giving me her word left me without any doubt that she would do her utmost to achieve these ends. The day passed as usual until Raphael returned, about six.

'Come along!' he said brusquely to Omphale, 'are you ready?'

'Yes, Father . . .'

'We must go! We must go immediately!'

'Allow me to embrace my companions.'

'That isn't necessary,' said the monk, pulling her by the arm. 'Someone is waiting for you – follow me!'

Then she asked if she should bring her clothes.

'Nothing, nothing!' exclaimed Raphael; 'doesn't everything belong to the house? You no longer have need of any of it!'

Then, attempting to take back his words in the fashion of one who has said too much: 'All these clothes are useless to you now. You shall have some made to your own measurements, and they'll suit you a lot better.'

I asked the monk if he would allow me to accompany Omphale as far as the door, but he answered with such a hard and surly glance that I recoiled in fear without repeating my request. As she left, our unhappy companion looked at me with anxious, tear-filled eyes; and as soon as she was gone all three of us abandoned ourselves to the sorrow we felt over this separation. Half an hour later Antonin came to take us down to supper. A further hour passed before Raphael appeared. He was unusually agitated, and often spoke to the others in low tones. But everything else continued in the accepted manner. I noticed, however, as Omphale had already warned me, that we were dismissed at an earlier hour and that the monks – who drank infinitely more than was their custom – excited their desires but never permitted their consummation. What conclusions was it possible to draw from such facts? I mention them now because one seems to notice everything on such occasions; but at the time I hadn't the courage to interpret their meaning. Perhaps you, Madame, may not be so surprised at the circumstances as I was then.

We waited four days for news of Omphale, persuaded at one

moment that she would never break the vow she had made, and convinced the following instant that the cruel precautions they must have taken with her had removed every possibility of her being useful to us. At last we despaired of her altogether and our anxiety increased in intensity. On the fourth day we were ordered down to supper as usual, but what was our surprise to see a new companion entering by another door just as we appeared in ours.

'Here is the girl whom the society has chosen to replace our last departure!' said Raphael, 'be so good, ladies, as to live with her as you possibly can.' Then turning towards me: 'You are the eldest in the class, Sophie, and I elevate you to the position of room-mistress. You know your duties – be sure to perform them carefully.'

I would have liked to refuse, but was unable to, being perpetually obliged to sacrifice my inclinations and my will to those of these villainous men. So I curtseyed and promised to do everything to his satisfaction.

Then they removed the little cloak and the veils which covered the head and shoulders of our new companion, and we saw a young girl of fifteen, with the most delicate and interesting features. Her eyes, although wet with tears, were superb. She lifted them most graciously towards all of us, and I can honestly say that never in my life have I seen more touching glances. Thick ash-blond hair floated round her shoulders in natural curls. She had fresh, rosy-red lips, held her head with dignity, and there was something so completely seductive in her that it was impossible to look at her without feeling drawn involuntarily towards her. We soon learned from her (I insert the details here, in order to keep everything concerning her in one place) that she was called Octavie, and was the daughter of an important merchant living in Lyons. She had been educated at Paris and was on her way home with a governess when they were attacked, at night, between Auxerre and Vermenton. She had been kidnapped and brought to this house without ever discovering what had happened to the carriage and her woman companion. After that she had been locked up, alone, in a low-ceilinged room. There, for an hour, she abandoned herself to despair; at the end of which time without a single word having been said by any of the monks she was brought to join us.

Faced with such charms, our four libertines were in ecstasy for a moment. But they only had strength to admire what stood before them, for the empire of beauty commands respect even in the most wicked and profligate of men – who cannot violate it without experiencing remorse. Nevertheless, monsters such as those with whom we had to deal languish little under such restraints: 'Come along, mademoiselle,' said the Superior, 'come along and let us see, I pray you, if the rest of your charms correspond with those nature has so generously scattered over your features.'

And as this beautiful girl showed signs of being troubled, as she blushed without really understanding what was said to her, the brutal Antonin seized her by the arm and shouted, with oaths and exclamations too indecent for repetition: 'Don't you understand then, you finical little creature, don't you understand that what you have been told to do is to strip yourself stark naked this very instant . . . ' Fresh tears were followed by further resistance . . . But Clément, grabbing hold of her, tore away within a minute everything which had veiled the modesty of this interesting creature. Those charms of Octavie, previously concealed by decency, were even more beautiful than those which custom allowed to be shown. Never has a whiter skin been seen, never such fortunate contours. But all this innocence, all this freshness and delicacy, were quickly to become the prey of a group of barbarians. It seemed that nature had showered countless favours only that they might be destroyed by the insensate beasts who held us in captivity.

A circle was formed round her and, just as I had done, she was obliged to cover it in every sense. Antonin, burning with lust, could not resist a cruel attack on such budding charms. But his worship was brief, and the incense smoked at the feet of the god . . . Raphael saw that it was time to think of more serious things. For his own part he was incapable of waiting, so he seized the victim and placed her according to his taste. Not succeeding so well as he might, he begged Clément to hold her for him. Octavie wept, but no one heard. Fire burned bright in the eyes of this abominable Italian. Master of the fortress he was about to storm, he considered his avenues of approach only the better to anticipate every resistance. Neither ruse nor any other form of preparation was employed. The enormous disproportion between the assailant and the rebel in no way interfered with his conquest. A heart-rending cry from the victim announced her defeat. But nothing softened her proud conqueror. The more she appeared to beg for mercy, the more ferociously did he press upon her; and, like myself, the wretched girl was ignominiously soiled without ceasing to be a virgin.

'Never were laurels more difficult to win,' said Raphael, as he puts himself to rights. 'I thought, for the first time in my life, that I was about to fail.'

'Let me take her over from here!' exclaimed Antonin, without letting her get up. 'There is more than a single breach in the rampart, and you've only taken one of them.'

As he spoke he advanced proudly into combat, and within a minute was master of the situation. Fresh sobs could be heard . . .

'Praise be to God!' said this horrible monster, 'I would have doubted my victory if I hadn't heard the cries of the vanquished. Moreover, I only esteem my triumph when it is drawn at the cost of tears.'

'To be truthful,' said Jérôme as he came forward, a bundle of twigs in his hand, 'neither shall I disturb this sweet posture, for it is perfectly suited to my designs.'

He looked, he touched, he felt. Then a frightful whistling noise echoed through the air. The beautiful flesh changed colour. The brilliant red of carnation mingled with the glow of lilies. Thus it is that something which in moderation might perhaps enliven a moment of love becomes, with incessant repetition, a crime against its laws. Nothing could stop the perfidious monk. The more the pupil wept, the greater each explosion of her master's severity . . . Every part was treated in the same manner, not a single portion of the flesh beneath him obtaining the slightest mercy. Soon this entire body was covered with the imprints of his barbarity; and it was upon these bleeding traces of his odious pleasures that this unspeakable man extinguished, at last, the fire which burned within him.

'I shall be more gentle than my brothers,' exclaimed Clément as he seized the beautiful creature in his arms and glued an impure kiss on her coral lips . . . 'Here is the temple in which I shall sacrifice!'

He inflamed himself further by implanting several fresh kisses upon that adorable mouth – a mouth which might have been formed by Venus herself. Then he forced the miserable girl to submit to those infamies which he found so delectable; and the happy organ of pleasure, the sweetest asylum of love, was soiled at last with horrors.

The remainder of the evening passed in the manner you already know. But the beauty, the pathetic youth of this girl, so increasingly inflamed the monsters that their atrocities redoubled; and it was satiety, much more than pity, which finally enabled the poor creature to retire to our room, where she was able to rest for a few hours in that quiet she so greatly needed. I should at least have liked to be able to console her on this first night. Obliged, however, to spend it with Antonin, it was myself who needed help. Unfortunately I seemed more ardently to excite the revolting desires of this debauchee than any other of the girls, and consequently there had been few weeks when I did not pass four or five nights in his room.

The following morning when I returned to our quarters I found my new comrade in tears. I repeated all that Omphale had once said to me under similar circumstances in an effort to calm her; but my good intentions were not successful. It is not at all easy to console anyone for such a sudden change of fate. Moreover, this young creature was blessed with considerable gifts of piety, of virtue, honour and sensitivity which could only make her feel more keenly the cruelty of her situation. Raphael, who was much taken with her, saw to it that she spent several nights in succession with him. And little by little she comforted herself in her misfortunes, just as we had done, with the hope that one day she would see them end. Omphale had had good reason to tell me that seniority had nothing to do with the granting of discharges. These were dictated solely by the caprice of the monks and were just as likely to be presented after eight days as after twenty years. Octavie had been with us less than six weeks when Raphael came to tell her that she was due to leave us . . . She made us the same promises as Omphale had done and disappeared in the same manner – without our ever finding out what had become of her.

We remained about a month without any replacement. It was during this interval that, like Omphale, I had reason to be persuaded that we were not the only girls who inhabited the house – and that there was doubtless another building which held a similar number to our own. Omphale had only suspected such a possibility. But my own experience, which was quite an adventure, absolutely confirmed my suspicions. This is how it happened. I had just spent the night with Raphael, and, according to custom, was leaving him about seven o'clock in the morning, when a Brother, equally as old and disgusting as ours – but whom I had never before seen – suddenly appeared in the corridor with a tall girl of eighteen or twenty. She seemed to me very beautiful, and would have been an attractive model for any artist. Raphael, who was to take me back, dawdled in his cell; and it so happened that I suddenly found myself face to face with this girl – whom the Brother was at an absolute loss to hide from my eyes.

'Where are you taking this creature?' demanded the Superior, furiously.

'Into your room, Reverend Father,' answered this abominable Mercury. 'Your Grace forgets that he gave me orders to do so yesterday evening.'

'I said it was to be at nine o'clock!'

'At seven o'clock, Monseigneur. You told me you wanted to see her before Mass.'

While this was going on I considered my companion – who was looking at me with the same astonishment.

'Ah, well, it doesn't matter,' said Raphael as he took me back into his room followed by the girl.

'Listen, Sophie,' he said, having closed the door and instructed the Brother to wait, 'this girl holds the same position in another tower as you do in yours – she is room-mistress. There is no inconvenience in our two senior girls being acquainted with each other, and so that your introduction shall be all the more complete, Sophie, I am going to show you Marianne completely nude.'

This Marianne, who seemed to me a very impudent and shameless sort of girl, undressed on the instant; and Raphael, ordering me to excite his desires, submitted her before my eyes to those pleasures he preferred best: 'That's just what I was in need of,' said the infamous creature as soon as he was satisfied. 'It is sufficient for me to have spent the night with a girl to make me want another in the morning. Nothing is so insatiable as these tastes of ours. The more we indulge them, the more they clamour for satisfaction. And although a man always does very much the same kind of things, he ceaselessly imagines fresh attractions in a new partner. The moment satiety extinguishes our desire for one partner is the same moment that libertinage fans the bright flame of lust for another. You two girls have our confidence – therefore hold your tongues. You may go now, Sophie. The Brother will take you back. As for me, I have a new mystery to celebrate with your companion.'

Octavie was shortly replaced by a little twelve year old peasant, fresh and pretty, but much inferior to her predecessor. Within two years I was the sole member remaining from the original company. Florette and Cornélie had left in their turn, each swearing, as Omphale had done, to send me news of themselves, and neither of them succeeding any better than that unfortunate young woman. Both were replaced – Florette by a fifteen year old from Dijon, plump and chubby, with nothing to commend her but her freshness and her age; and Cornélie by a singularly beautiful girl belonging to an eminently respectable Autun family. This last young woman, who was sixteen, had fortunately stolen Antonin's heart from me – I say 'fortunately', but I very quickly realised that if I had been removed from the good graces of this libertine, I was equally on the eve of losing my credit with the others. The unreliability of these wretches made me tremble for my fate. I saw well enough that the situation announced my discharge. And, realising only too clearly that this cruel permission to leave was nothing other than a sentence of death, I was, for some moments, considerably alarmed. I say for some moments! Yet, unfortunate as I was, why should I cling to life when the greatest blessing that could happen to me would be to leave it?

Such reflections comforted me, and helped me await my end with so much resignation that I employed no means whatever to regain my credit. Ill luck began to overwhelm me, and there wasn't an instant when one or another of them didn't complain about me, not a day when I wasn't punished. I prayed to heaven and awaited my sentence. I was perhaps on the eve of receiving it when the hand of providence, weary of tormenting me in the same manner, tore me from this new abyss only to replunge me, shortly, into another. But let me not anticipate events. First I must tell you how we were at last delivered from the hands of these notorious debauchees.

It was necessary that the frightful example of vice triumphant should be maintained, even in the present circumstances, just as it had always been throughout each event in my life. It was written that those who had tormented me, humiliated me, chained me in irons, should ceaselessly receive, before my very eyes, the benefits of their criminal activities – as if providence had taken upon itself the task of showing me the inutility of virtue. Such deadly lessons, however, have never been successful in correcting me; and should I once more escape the sword suspended above my head, they will not prevent me from remaining the slave of this divinity of my heart.

One morning when we didn't expect him, Antonin appeared in our room and announced to us that the Reverend Father Raphael, relative and protégé of the Pope, had just been named by His Holiness as General of the Order of Saint Francis.

'And I, my children,' he added, 'have been promoted to the position of Superior at Lyons. Two new Fathers will immediately replace us in this house. They may arrive today. We do not know them and it is possible that, instead of retaining you here, they may send you back to your homes. But whatever your fate, I advise you, for your own good as well as for the honour of the two colleagues whom we are leaving here, to conceal all details as to our conduct and to admit nothing but what it is impossible to deny.'

Having received such wonderful news we found ourselves at a loss in refusing the monk what he appeared to desire. So we promised him everything, and the libertine made his goodbyes to all four of us. The end of misfortune being in sight we withstood the final blows without complaint. We refused him nothing. And when he left it was to separate himself once and for all from all of us. Dinner was served, and two hours later Father Clément entered our rooms. He was accompanied by two gentlemen, reverend both in age and in appearance.

'Admit, Father,' one of them said to Clément, 'admit that these debauchees are horrible, and that it is most singular that Heaven has suffered them so long.'

Clément humbly agreed with everything; but attempted to excuse himself by explaining that neither he nor his colleagues were responsible for any of the circumstances – they had found the place in the state in which they were now handing it over. To he honest, he explained, the subjects varied, but they had found even this variety established on their arrival and had done nothing more than follow the usage indicated by their predecessors.

'So be it,' replied the Father who seemed to be the new Superior, 'so let it be; but let us quickly suppress this execrable debauchery – a debauchery which would be revolting even in people of the outside world. I leave you to ponder,' he added, 'just what it should mean to those whose lives have been given up to religion.'

Then he asked us all what we wished to do. Everyone replied that she wanted to return either to her town or to her family.

'It shall be so, my children,' said the monk. 'I shall give each of you the sum necessary to make this possible; but it will be necessary for you to leave one after another, with an interval of two days between each departure. You must also leave alone, on foot, and never reveal anything of what has happened in this house.'

We swore what he required of us, but the new Superior was not content with our promises . . . He also requested us to draw near to the Sacrament. None of us refused; and when we had knelt at the foot of the altar he made us take an oath that we would, throughout our lives, conceal everything that had happened in the monastery. I gave my word with the others; and if I have broken it in so far as you are concerned, Madame, it is because I accepted the spirit, rather than the letter of this vow insisted on by the good priest. His object, of course, was that no complaint should be brought against his order. But I feel quite certain that, although I have freely entrusted you with the details of my adventures, nothing troublesome will result for any of these good Fathers.

My companions were the first to leave; and as we had been separated since the moment of the new Superior's arrival – being also forbidden to make any appointments to meet – we never saw each other again. I had asked to go to Grenoble and was given two louis to take me there. Putting on the clothes I had worn when I arrived at this place, I found in one of the pockets the eight other louis which still remained to me from my previous experiences. Then, full of satisfaction at being able to fly once and for all from that terrible refuge of vice – and in such a protected and unexpected manner – I set off into the forest. I soon found myself once more on the road to Auxerre, at the same point at which I had left it to throw myself into such a sea of trouble. It was just three years after that piece of foolishness – which is to say that I was now twenty-five, or would be in a few weeks.

My first care was to fall on my knees to beg fresh pardon of God for all the involuntary faults I had committed. And I prayed with much deeper contrition that I had ever felt when stretched before the defiled altars of that infamous house I had left with such joy. Tears of remorse began to stream from my eyes . . .

'Alas,' I said to myself, 'I was pure when, long ago, I left this same road, led by a principle of devotion which proved so fatally deceptive . . . And just look at the sad state I'm in now!'

These gloomy reflections were softened somewhat by the pleasure I felt in knowing myself to be free, and I continued on my way. In order to avoid wearying you any longer, Madame, with such details as must tax your patience I shall in future – if you agree – describe only such events as taught me some salutary lesson or made some definite change in the course of my life.

While staying for some days at Lyons, I happened to glance through the pages of a foreign newspaper belonging to the woman at whose house I was lodging. You can imagine my surprise when its pages informed me that once again crime had been rewarded – that one of the principal authors of my sufferings had attained the pinnacle of fame. Rodin, that villainous creature who had punished me so cruelly for preventing a projected murder, obliged to leave France – doubtless for having committed others – had just been appointed first surgeon to the King of Sweden, and at a very considerable salary. 'May the wicked wretch continue fortunate,' I thought, 'since providence seems to wish it. As for yourself, you miserable creature, you can suffer alone and in silence, since it is written that tribulation and pain should be the frightful portion of virtue!'

At the end of three days I left Lyons to travel on to Dauphiné, filled with the wild hope that at least a little good fortune might await me in that province. I had scarcely covered more than two leagues from Lyons, walking, as usual, my only luggage being a couple of chemises and some handkerchiefs which I kept in a pocket, when I met an old woman who sadly came up to me and begged my charity. Compassionate by nature, and never having experienced a single joy in the world comparable to that of obliging others, I immediately brought out my purse with the intention of taking from it a few pieces of money to give to this woman. But the unworthy creature, more prompt than myself – although at first I had taken her for an old and decrepit individual – felled me instantly with a vigorous blow in the stomach. By the time I managed to get to my feet she was a hundred paces away, surrounded by four rascals whose menacing gestures warned me of the dangers that faced me should I dare to approach them . . .

'Oh! just heaven,' I cried bitterly, 'is it then impossible for any virtuous impulse to find birth in me without my immediately being punished with all the most cruel and fearful misfortunes in the universe!'

At this terrifying moment all my courage was ready to abandon me. Today I beg pardon of heaven, but at the time I am speaking of revolt was terribly near my heart. Two dreadful courses lay open before me – either I could join the rogues who had so cruelly injured me, or return to Lyons and give myself up to a life of prostitution . . . God gave me grace to resist; and, although the hope which was thus re-illumined in my heart proved merely the dawn of even more terrible adversities, I still thank Him for having sustained me through it all. The chain of misfortunes which takes me today, innocent, to the scaffold, will result in nothing but my death. But the choice of any other way of life would have brought me shame, remorse, ignominy – and death is far less cruel to me than these.

I continued on my way, having decided to sell what few things I had at Vienne so that I might proceed to Grenoble. Thus I trudged sadly along until, just over half a mile from the town, I saw on the plain at the right of the road two men on horseback, who were trampling a third beneath their horses' hooves. Leaving him at last for dead, they galloped quickly away . . . This terrible scene moved me to the point of tears . . .

'Alas,' I said to myself, 'here is someone more unfortunate than I have been, for at least I retain my health and my strength. At least I can earn my living, while this man, if he is not wealthy but in similar circumstances to my own – well, he will be crippled for the remainder of his life! And what will become of him?'

However much I should have smothered these sentiments of pity, however much I had been cruelly punished in the past for giving way to the dictates of such emotion, I could not resist them. So I went up to the dying man and made him breathe a little spirit which I carried with me. He opened his eyes, and his first movements were those of gratitude. They seemed to beg me to continue my attentions, and I tore up one of my chemises that I might bind his wounds – it was one of the few things left me which I might sell so as to prolong my life. I tore it to shreds for this man, staunching the blood which flowed from his injuries and making him drink a little wine that I carried in a flask so that I might renew my strength for walking during moments of exhaustion. I washed his bruises with what remained of it.

At length the unfortunate creature recovered something of his strength and his spirits. Although he was on foot and only lightly dressed, he did not look poor. Moreover, he possessed some quite valuable things – rings, a watch, and other jewels all badly damaged by his adventure. Finally, when he was able to speak, he asked who might be the gracious angel who lent him aid, and what he might do to prove his gratitude. Still being simple enough to believe that a soul enslaved by thankfulness would be entirely devoted to me, I thought I might safely enjoy the sweet pleasure of sharing my tears with one who had shed his own in the shelter of my arms. I told him all that had befallen me and he listened with interest. When I described to him the final catastrophe, disclosing my terrible poverty, he looked at me and exclaimed: 'How happy I am to be alive and able to acknowledge all you have done for me! My name is Dalville, and I am the owner of a very beautiful castle in the mountains about forty-five miles from here. I can offer you a home there, if you will come with me. And in order that such a proposal need not frighten you or offend against your sense of delicacy, I shall immediately explain the way in which you can be useful to me. I am married, you see, and my wife has need of a trustworthy woman to attend her. Recently we had to dismiss a very bad servant, and I offer you her place.'

Humbly I thanked my protector and asked him how such a man as he had risked travelling alone, without attendants, thus leaving himself open to such ill-treatment by ruffians as he had actually suffered.

'Lusty, young and vigorous, it has always been my habit to travel to Vienne in this manner. My health and my purse both gain equally by it. Nevertheless, I need not trouble myself over finance, for I'm very wealthy – as you shall see if you will do me the kindness of coming home with me. Those two men with whom you saw me having a tussle are two petty lordlings of the district with nothing whatever to their names except their capes and their swords. Which is as good as saying that both of them are rascals. Last week I won a hundred louis from them in a house at Vienne, but I didn't receive even the thirtieth part of this from them. I accepted their promise of payment, met them today, and asked for what they owed me . . . and you have seen how they paid me!'

I deplored with this honest gentleman the double misfortune to which he had fallen victim; then he suggested that we should be getting on our way.

'I feel a little better now,' said Dalville, ' – thanks to your care. But night is coming on, so we must reach an inn I know about two leagues from here. We can borrow horses there in the morning, and probably reach my castle by the same evening.'

Absolutely in favour of profiting by this help which Heaven seemed to have sent me, I helped Dalville to walk, sustaining him on our way. Leaving all known roads we set out across country, following footpaths which led, as the bird flies, towards the Alps. After covering nearly two leagues we found the inn which Dalville had mentioned. We had supper together, gaily, and observing all propriety. After which he commended me to the landlady, who arranged for me to sleep near her. And next day, riding two hired mules and escorted by a servant from the tavern, we reached the frontiers of Dauphiné and directed our steps towards the mountains. Still suffering from the wounds he had received, Dalville was not in a state to withstand the entire journey. I was not at all sorry about this for, being unaccustomed to such a manner of travelling, I found myself equally indisposed. We halted at Virieu, where my guide paid me the same attentions and the same respect as hitherto. On the following morning we continued on our journey, always in the same direction, and at four o'clock we reached the foothills of the mountains. Here the road became almost impassable. Dalville instructed the muleteer not to leave me, in case of accident, and we threaded our way through the gorges. We seemed to do nothing but twist and turn and climb for about four leagues and then we had left every human abode and pathway so far behind that I felt we must be at the very edge of the world. Despite myself a slight sense of inquietude began to take hold of me. Weaving my way through these inaccessible rocks I was reminded of my detours in the forest which surrounded the monastery of Sainte-Marie-des-Bois. And the aversion I had learned to feel for all isolated spots caused me to tremble at this one. At last we perceived a castle perched on the edge of a terrifying precipice. It seemed to hang over the edge of a steep wall of rock, and had every aspect of a habitation for ghosts rather than for flesh and blood members of human society. Moreover, although we could see the castle, no road seemed to lead to it. The one we followed was very stony and much frequented by goats. Nevertheless it led to this edifice, but by infinite detours.

'There is my house,' exclaimed Dalville, noticing my expression as I gazed at it. I expressed my surprise that he should inhabit such a desolate place, and he replied – but quite harshly – that a man lived where he could. I was as much shocked as frightened by the tone of his voice, for nothing goes unnoticed in misfortune. The slightest modulation or inflexion in the voice of those upon whom one depends is able, during such periods, to stifle or to revive one's hope. But, as it

was too late to withdraw, I decided to take no notice of his attitude. At
last, after much twisting and turning in our climb round this ancient
ruin, we suddenly found ourselves directly in front of it. Dalville
dismounted from his mule and, asking me to do likewise, returned
them to the lackey, paid him, and ordered him to return to the inn. A
ceremony which, under the circumstances, displeased me very
considerably.

Dalville noticed my disquietude.

'What's the matter with you, Sophie?' he said as we walked towards
his dwelling. 'You haven't left France. This castle is on the border of
Dauphiné, and you are still in your own country!'

'That may be so, monsieur,' I replied, 'but how did you come to
establish yourself in such a cut-throat's retreat?'

'Cut-throat's retreat?' bandied Dalville, looking at me slyly as we
approached the building; 'no, it isn't quite that, my child – but neither
is it the home of perfectly respectable people.'

'Ah, monsieur,' I replied, 'you make me shudder! Where are you
taking me?'

'I am taking you to work for some coiners of counterfeit money,
slut!' he said, as he seized hold of me and forced me over a drawbridge
which had been lowered on our arrival, and which was raised immediately afterwards.

'Here we are!' he added, as soon as we were in the courtyard. Then,
showing me a wide and extremely deep cistern neighbouring on the
gate where two chained and naked women continually moved a
wheel which drew water to feed a reservoir, 'Do you see this pit?' he
continued, ' – these are your companions, and this will be your work.
On condition that you work twelve hours a day turning this wheel, you
will be given six ounces of black bread and a plate of beans once in
twenty-four hours. Moreover, you will be well and regularly beaten
each time you attempt to rest. As for liberty, you can renounce all
thought of that, for never will you see the sky again. As soon as you are
dead you will be thrown into this hole which you can see beside the
well – on top of thirty or forty other bodies which are there already –
and your work will be taken over by someone else!'

'In heaven's name, monsieur,' I cried, throwing myself at Dalville's
feet, 'don't you remember that I saved your life, and that in a moment
of gratitude you offered me happiness? Surely I have a right to expect
better than this!'

'And what, I beg you, do you mean by this feeling of gratitude – this
feeling by which you imagine you hold me captive? Such wretched
creatures as yourself should reason better than this! What did you do

when you helped me? You had the choice of continuing on your way, or of coming over to assist me. You chose the latter, inspired by some profound emotion springing from deep within your heart . . . That in itself is a kind of pleasure, so how in the devil's name can you claim that I should be obliged to reward you for pleasures which you grant to yourself? And how could you possibly let it enter your head that a man like myself, swimming in gold, surrounded by opulence, and more than a millionaire – a man who is about to move to Venice that he may enjoy life at his ease – how could you come to the conclusion that a man such as this should deign to lower himself by admitting any kind of debt to a miserable little wretch like you!

'And even if you did save my life, I still don't owe you anything, for you acted only in your own interests. Get to work, you slave – get to work! And learn that civilisation may overthrow nature's institutions, but never her rights! Originally she created strong beings and weak beings. Her intention was that the latter should always be subordinate to the former, as the lamb is to the lion, the insect to the elephant. When we come to man, however, it is skill and intelligence which determine the position of individuals. Rank is no longer determined by physical strength, but it can be, and is, determined by wealth. The richest man has become the strongest, the poor man the weakest. The priority of the strong over the weak was always one of the laws of nature. Moreover, she is indifferent as to whether the power of the strong over the weak is by reason of their wealth or by reason of their physical strength. And she is equally indifferent as to whether this power crushes those who are physically weak, or those who are merely poor.

'As for those feelings of gratitude which you claim man should feel, Sophie, nature ignores them. It was never within the reasoning of her laws that the pleasure one feels in obliging another should become a cause, for the man who benefits by such obligation, to relax his rights upon the other. Have you found these feelings anywhere amongst the animals who serve us? Since I dominate you by means of my wealth and my strength, would it be natural for me to abandon my rights over you simply because you enjoyed helping me, or because your own peculiar reasoning suggested that you would find redemption in aiding me?

'And even if the service had been rendered by an equal to an equal, never would the pride of an elevated soul allow itself to be degraded by the sentiment of gratitude. The man who receives from another is always humiliated in the receiving – and is not this very humiliation sufficient repayment for the service rendered? Is it not true that the pride of the helper delights in the strength of being able to assist? And is any other reward really necessary for the man or woman who obliges? Besides, if such obligation, by humbling the recipient, should become a burden to him, by what right would you force him to bear it? Why should it be necessary for me to allow myself to feel a sense of humiliation every time I meet the glance of whoever has performed me some such service?

'Thus ingratitude instead of being a vice is truly the virtue of proud intellects – just as surely as kindness is that of weak ones. The slave preaches the virtues of kindness and humility to his master because as a slave he has need of them; but the master, better guided by nature and his passions, has no need to devote himself to anything excepting those things which serve or please him. Be as kind as you wish, if you enjoy such things – but don't demand any reward for having had your pleasure.'

At these words, to which Dalville gave me no time to reply, two footmen seized me, stripped me on his orders, and chained me alongside my two companions. I had no choice but to work with them immediately, not even being allowed to rest after the tiring journey I had made. Scarcely had I been at this wheel for fifteen minutes than the entire gang of counterfeiters – who had just finished their day's work – crowded round to examine me, headed by their chief. Every one of them heaped sarcasm and impertinence on me, having noticed the dishonourable mark of the branding iron which I innocently bore upon my body. They approached me, touched and handled me brutally everywhere, and criticised with biting pleasantry every portion of my anatomy.

This painful scene over, they withdrew a little distance. Dalville then seized a horse-whip which was always kept near us and, with all the strength of his arm, gave me five or six lashes over every part of my body.

'This is how you will be treated here, you lazy slut,' he said as the lash fell. 'This is what you will receive every time you are unfortunate enough to fail in your duty. These, of course, are not because you have failed, but only to show you how I treat those who do.'

Each blow tore away strips of my skin; and, never having felt such infernal pain, either in the hands of Bressac or in those of the barbarous monks, I screamed loudly and shrilly as I struggled in my chains. Such writhings and twistings, and such cries of agony, only aroused the mocking laughter of the monsters who were watching me; and I had the cruel satisfaction of learning that, if there are men who, ruled by vengeance or by a vile sense of the voluptuous are able to enjoy the pain of another, there yet remain individuals so barbarously organised that they relish the same delights without any other motive than the gratification of pride or the most terrifying curiosity. It seems, therefore, that man is naturally wicked. He is so in the delirium of his passions, and almost equally so even when they are calm. But in either case the sufferings of his brothers can become an execrable pleasure in his eyes.

Three dark holes, each separated from the other and locked like prisons, were close to the pit. One of the footmen who had chained me indicated the one I was to occupy and I withdrew to it, having received my destined portion of water, beans and bread. There, at leisure, I was able to abandon myself completely to the horror of my situation.

'Alas,' I said to myself, 'is it possible that there are men barbarous enough to stifle within themselves any sentiment of gratitude, that virtue to which I would abandon myself so gladly if ever an honest soul gave me the chance of feeling its promptings? How can it be so despised by men? And is the man who smothers it so inhumanly anything other than a monster?'

I was occupied in such reflections, mingling them with my tears, when suddenly the door of my cell was opened. It was Dalville. Without saying a word, and in absolute silence, he placed his candle on the ground and threw himself on me with the ferocity of a wild beast. Repulsing with blows my attempts at self-defence and scorning my pleas for mercy, he subjected me to his desires and satisfied himself brutally. Then he took up his light and, locking the door, disappeared.

'Is it possible to carry outrage further?' I asked myself. 'And what difference can there be between such a man and the most savage animals of the forest?'

The sun arose without my having enjoyed a single moment of rest. Our cells were opened, we were rechained to the wheel, and our sad labours recommenced. My companions were two girls of between twenty-five and thirty who, although brutalised by suffering and deformed by excess of physical pain, still retained the vestiges of beauty. Their figures were pretty and well turned and one of them still possessed superb hair. A depressing conversation acquainted me with the fact that they had both been, at different times, mistresses of Dalville. One at Lyons, the other at Grenoble. He had brought them both to this horrible retreat where they had continued for several years on the same kind of footing. Then, as recompense for the pleasures they had brought him, he condemned them to this humiliating work.

I learned from them that he had, at the present moment, a charming mistress who, more fortunate than they had been, would probably accompany him to Venice – to which he was on the eve of moving, if the considerable sums which he had recently sent to Spain should produce the bills of exchange he required for Italy. For he did not wish to take his gold there, preferring to send it to agents in a country other than the one in which he planned to reside, as it was all in false coinage. By these means he was rich in whatever place he wished to live, but on papers drawn on a different country. Thus his manoeuvres remained free of discovery, while his fortune remained solidly established. It was, nevertheless, possible that he might lose everything in an instant; and the retreat he was mediating depended absolutely on the success of this last transaction – in which the greater part of his wealth was compromised. If Cadiz accepted his piastres and his louis, sending him in return acceptable bills made payable at Venice, then he would be happy for the remainder of his life. But if the deception was discovered then he risked being denounced and hanged as he deserved.

'Alas,' I said to myself when I learned these particulars, '– but providence must be merciful this time. She will never let a monster like this succeed, and all three of us will be avenged.'

At midday we were given two hours in which to rest, and we profited by it to the extent of going separately into our own chambers where we ate and regained our breath. At two o'clock we were chained again to the wheel, which we turned until night fell. Never were we allowed to enter the castle. The reason why we were kept thus naked during five months in the year was by reason of the insupportable heat and the excessive work which we did. And besides, as my companions assured me, in this state we were best prepared to receive the blows which, from time to time, our surly master came to bestow on us. During winter we were given trousers and skin-tight waistcoats which, by their very clinging fit, exposed us just as well to the blows of the butcherous Dalville.

During my first day there he did not appear; but towards midnight he came to me and behaved in precisely the same fashion as on the previous night. I tried to take advantage of this moment by begging him to soften my lot.

'And by what right do you make such a request?' this barbarian said to me. 'Is it because I have momentarily chosen to indulge my fancies with you? But am I kneeling at your feet and pleading for favours for which you might demand some sort of payment? I am asking nothing of you . . . I take, and I do not see why this right which I enjoy over you should result in my abstention from any others which I may hold. There is no love in my intercourse with you, for that is an emotion which my heart has never known. I serve myself with a woman by necessity, just as I use a chamberpot for a different need; but I grant no rights to these creatures, who are subjected to my desires either by my money or by my authority. Nor do I dispense respect or tenderness. I owe what I take to myself alone, and I demand nothing of a woman but her submission. I do not see how that obliges me to offer her my gratitude You might just as well say that a robber who forcibly takes a man's purse in a wood owes that man some gratitude because he has profited financially by his superior strength. It is the same when one outrages a woman. Such an outrage may justify a second attack, but is never sufficient reason for granting her any sort of compensation.'

Dalville, who by this time had reached his culmination, abruptly left me as soon as he had finished speaking. But he plunged me into new reflections which, as you may well imagine, were not to his advantage. That evening he came to watch us at work, and finding that we had not furnished the normal quantity of water, he seized his cruel horse-whip and lashed the three of us until we bled. Yet, although he spared me no more than the others, he did not fail to return the same night in order to behave in the usual manner. Showing him the wounds with which he had covered me, I was bold enough to remind him of the time when I had torn my linen into strips so as to bind his own injuries. But Dalville, continuing with his selfish pleasures, replied to my complaints only with a dozen blows mingled with vituperation and invective. And, following his habit, he left me immediately he had achieved physical satisfaction. This programme was followed for almost a month, after which the butcher was gracious enough no longer to expose me to the shocking torture of letting him take what he was so little fitted to receive. My life scarcely changed, however, for I experienced neither more nor less as regards moments of tranquillity, and neither more nor less in the way of cruel treatment.

A year sped by in this painful manner when news began to circulate, not only that Dalville's fortune was made and that he had received, for payment in Venice, the immense amount of notes he desired, but also that he had been asked for several million more in false coinage – for which, according to his wishes, he would receive bills of exchange payable at Venice. The success of such a criminal could never have been more magnificent or more unexpected. He would leave with over a million ready at hand and with much more to come! Such was the new lesson which providence set before me, and such was her latest method of once more attempting to convince me that prosperity waited on crime and misfortune on virtue . . .

Dalville prepared to leave, and on the midnight of his last day at the castle he came to see me – a thing which had not happened for a long time. He told me of his good fortune and announced his departure. I threw myself at his feet and begged him earnestly to set me free, asking him to give me just a little money to get me as far as Grenoble.

'At Grenoble,' he exclaimed, 'you would denounce me!'

'Very well, monsieur,' I said, soaking his knees with my tears, 'I give you my word that I will not set foot in the place. The better to convince you of my sincerity, and if you will deign to take me with you to Venice, perhaps I may find there hearts which are less hard than those in my own country. Moreover, I swear to you by everything that I hold most sacred, once we are there I shall never trouble you again . . .'

'I have no intention of helping you in any way whatsoever – I wouldn't give you even one solitary coin,' replied this worthless wretch. 'All those things known as generosity or charity are so repugnant to my character that, even were I three times as rich as I am, I would never consent to give even a halfpenny to an indigent. My principles are based upon this rule and I shall never depart from it. The poverty-stricken are within the order of nature. In creating men of unequal strength she convinces us of her wish that this inequality should be preserved despite those modifications which civilisation effects in her laws. In civilisation the poor replace the physically weak, as I have already said – and to assist the poor is to disturb the established order. It means that one stands in opposition to nature, attempting to overthrow the equilibrium which lies at the base of her most sublime arrangements. The man who helps the poor works towards an equality which is dangerous to society. He encourages laziness and indolence, teaching the poor to steal from the rich – whenever it pleases the latter to refuse that assistance to which the former has become accustomed.'

'Oh, but these are hard principles, monsieur! Would you speak in this manner if you had not always been rich?'

'That is beside the point! I knew how to master my fate, to tread under my feet this phantom of virtue which leads either to the workhouse or to the gallows. I learned at an early age that religion, charity, and kindness were stumbling blocks to all who aimed at wealth and good fortune, and I consolidated my own on the debris of man's prejudice. It was by mocking law, both human and divine, by always sacrificing the feeble when they crossed my path, by abusing the good faith and the credulity of others, by ruining the poor and robbing the wealthy that I have attained the precipitous temple of the divinity I worship. Why didn't you imitate me? Your fortune was already in your hands! And has the chimerical virtue which you preferred above worldly success – has this virtue consoled you for all the sacrifices you have offered up to it? It is far too late to do anything about it now, wretched girl. All you can do is weep over the mistakes you have made;

and, suffering, try to find – if you can – something guarded by the phantoms you revere but which your credulity has lost you.'

With these cruel words Dalville threw himself upon me . . . But he filled me with such horror and his frightful maxims inspired so much hatred in me that I repulsed him with severity. He tried attempting force and, failing, compensated himself with cruelty. I was overwhelmed with blows, but still he did not triumph. His fire burned itself out without success and the tears of the insane creature avenged me at last for the outrages he had perpetrated.

The next day, before leaving, this vicious man presented us with a fresh scene of barbarity and cruelty which cannot be equalled by anything described in the annals of Andronicus, of Nero, of Wenceslas or Tiberius.

Everyone believed that his mistress was leaving with him. So he made her dress suitably. Then, at the moment when they were about to mount their horses, he led her over to us: 'There is your place, vile creature!' he exclaimed, as he ordered her to undress. 'I would like my comrades to remember me; therefore I am leaving them, as a token, the woman with whom they thought I was most infatuated. But since only three women are necessary here . . . and since I am about to travel along a dangerous road where my firearms will be useful, I am going to try out my pistols on one of you!'

As he said this he loaded one of them, holding it in turn to the breasts of each of the three women who rotated the wheel. Finally he addressed himself to one of these former mistresses: 'Go,' he shouted at her as he blew out her brains, ' – go and take news of me to the other world! Tell the devil that Dalville is the richest criminal on earth, and that he insolently defies, and equally, both the hands of heaven and those of hell.'

It was a horrible sight watching this poor creature, who did not die immediately but struggled a long time in her chains. The infamous villain observed it with delight, but finally had her removed in order to put his mistress in her place. This was because he wanted to see her turn the wheel a few times and to receive, under his hand, a dozen blows from his horse-whip. These atrocities achieved, the abominable man mounted his horse and, followed by two valets, disappeared for ever from our sight.

Everything changed from the day after Dalville's departure. His successor, a gentle and reasonable man, had us instantly released.

'This is not work for the weak and kindly sex,' he said to us benevolently. 'It is for animals to turn this machine! The profession we follow is criminal enough without our offending still further by our gratuitous atrocities the Supreme One who reigns on high.'

He established us in the castle, disinterestedly returned Dalville's mistress to her various household duties and gave my companion and me places in the workshop where we occupied ourselves in trimming the coins – which was a far less fatiguing job, and one for which we were recompensed with admirable rooms and excellent food. After a couple of months Dalville's successor – who was named Roland – acquainted us with the happy arrival of his colleague in Venice. He had already established himself there, realising his fortune, and was enjoying all the prosperity he had flattered himself he would find.

His successor should certainly have enjoyed the same kind of good fortune. But the unfortunate Roland was upright and of a kindly disposition, which qualities were quite sufficient for him promptly to be crushed. One day when tranquillity reigned over the castle – when, under the régime of this good master, the work, although criminal, was pleasurably and easily achieved – all at once the walls were beseiged. Unable to make use of the drawbridge our attackers scaled the moat, and before our men had even time to dream of defending themselves the house was filled with more than a hundred cavaliers of the horse-police. We were obliged to surrender. We were all chained like beasts, placed on horses, and taken to Grenoble.

'Oh, Heaven,' I thought, as we entered the town, 'here I am at last in the place where I had the folly to believe that happiness would be born for me!'

The trial of the counterfeiters soon came to an end. Every one of them was condemned to be hung. When my captors saw the mark of the branding iron on me they almost ceased to question me, and I was about to be condemned with the others. But I attempted to arouse some pity in a famous magistrate who dwelt in the city. He was the glory of all courts, a judge of integrity, a cherished citizen, and an enlightened philosopher whose celebrated and honourable name will for ever remain engraved, by his benevolence and humanity, on the walls of the temple of Memory! He listened to me . . . He did more, for convinced of my good faith and the truth of my misfortunes, he even consoled me with his own tears. Oh, greatest of men, to whom I owe my homage, grant to my heart the right to offer its thanks to you. The gratitude of an unfortunate such as I should not be burdensome to you; and the tribute I offer in honouring your warmth of heart will always remain one of the sweetest joys of my existence.

Monsieur S— actually became my advocate! My complaints were heard, my sobs penetrated the souls of those who listened, and my tears flowed over hearts which were certainly not made of steel, but which his generosity had completely opened to me. The general evidence presented by the criminals who were to be executed was in my favour, and thus strengthened the zeal of this man who had so wholeheartedly interested himself in my welfare. It was declared that I had been the prisoner of malefactors, and was thus innocent. Thus given a clean sheet and freed from all accusation of every kind, I had complete and absolute liberty to become whatever I wished. My protector increased these blessings by making a collection for me and I found myself in possession of nearly a hundred pistoles. At last I seemed to be seeing happiness in store for me, and my most deeply felt desires seemed about to be realised. I believed my misfortunes were over; but then it pleased providence once more to convince me that I still had far to travel.

On leaving prison I went to lodge at an inn which faced the Pont d'Isère. I was assured that I would be decently received in this house; and it was my intention, on the advice of Monsieur S—, to stay there for a while so that I might try and find work in the town. If I did not succeed I would return to Lyons with the letters of recommendation which he had so kindly given me.

Eating in this inn at what was known as the *table de l'hôte*, I noticed on the second day that I was being closely observed by a plump, well-dressed woman, who gave herself the title of Baroness. Examining her in my turn, I seemed to recognise her. Mutually we approached one another, and embraced like two people who know each other but cannot remember where they met. The rotund Baroness eventually took me aside and said: 'Am I mistaken, Sophie? Aren't you the girl I saved from the conciergerie ten years ago? And don't you remember la Dubois?'

Though little pleased by this discovery, I answered politely. But I was dealing with the most cunning and adroit woman in all France. There was no means of escaping her. La Dubois overwhelmed me with kindness and attention, telling me that she, like the other inhabitants of this city, had been most interested in my case but had not known at the time that it was I who was involved. Weak-willed, as usual, I let her take me to her room, where I told her of all my latest misfortunes.

'My dear friend,' she exclaimed as she embraced me again, 'if I wish to see you thus intimately, it is only to tell you that my fortune is made and all that I have is at your service!'

'Look!' she said, as she opened some caskets brimming with gold and diamonds, 'here are the fruits of my industry. If, like you, I had burned my incense at the feet of virtue, today I would either be hanged or in prison.'

'Oh, Madame,' I cried, 'if you obtained these things only by way of crime, providence, who always ends by being just, will not let you enjoy them for long . . .'

'There you are deceiving yourself,' said la Dubois, 'for you must not always suppose that providence is so partial to virtue. In your moment of temporary prosperity do not let yourself be plunged into such an error of reasoning. It is a matter of no importance in the maintenance of providence's laws that one man should be vicious while another adheres to virtue. She needs equal quantities of vice and virtue and is absolutely indifferent as to whether an individual chooses the one course or the other.

'Listen to me, Sophie – give me a little of your attention, for you are intelligent, and I think that in the long run I can convince you. It is not the choice which a man makes between vice and virtue which ultimately opens his door to happiness my dear; for virtue, like vice, is just a way of conducting oneself in the world. It is not a case of following either the one or the other but, rather, a question of following the common route. The man who strays from it is always wrong and liable to injure himself. In a world which was entirely virtuous I would advise you to be virtuous, because such conduct would then bring its natural recompense, happiness dancing infallible attendance upon it. But in a world totally corrupted I can never advise anything but vice. The man who doesn't follow in the same road as others inevitably perishes. Everything he meets will bump into him, contrariwise, and he will necessarily eventually be broken.

'It is in vain that our laws seek to re-establish order and to lead men back to virtue. Men are too vicious to attempt such a rehabilitation and too weak to succeed. Such laws may cause one momentarily to deviate from the beaten track, but they will never make him permanently leave it. When the common interests of men carry them forward into corruption, the man who would avoid becoming corrupted with the others will thus be fighting against the common interest. And what happiness can be expected by anyone who perpetually opposes the interests of others? Are you going to tell me that it is vice which opposes the general interest of mankind? I would grant you such a proposition if the world were composed equally of vicious and virtuous people, because, under such circumstances, the interests of one group would visibly conflict with those of the other. But this is no longer possible in a society which is corrupt from top to bottom. In such a society my vices exert their effects only upon others who are vicious, determining them to indulge in other and compensatory vices – thus all of us are content.

'The vibration becomes general, consisting of a multitude of shocks and mutual injuries whereby each one gains in an instant what he has just lost, thus finding himself in a perpetually happy position. Vice is only dangerous to virtue because, feeble and intimidated, she never dares to retaliate. But if virtue was banished from the face of the earth, vice, outraging only the vicious, would bother nobody. One vice might bring to light another, but in doing so it would not disturb virtue. And supposing anyone should object to this, stressing the good which results from virtue? That is merely another sophism, for the so called benefits of virtue have never served any but the weak, being useless to those whose strength and energy make them self-sufficient and who need but their own skill in order to redress the caprices of fate. How could you expect anything other than continual failure throughout your life, dear girl, when you have ceaselessly taken the contrary direction on the road which all men follow? If, like me, you had abandoned yourself whole-heartedly to the current, you would finally have arrived in port. Can the man who swims against the current arrive as quickly as he who swims with it? The one opposes nature; the other lets go and abandons himself to it! You are always prattling to me of providence; but wherein lies your proof that she loves order – and consequently virtue? Isn't she always presenting you with examples of her injustices and her irregularities? Is it because she has sent men not only war, but famine and pestilence, and because she has created a universe vicious in every aspect that you find her manifesting her extreme love of virtue? And why do you claim that vicious individuals displease her, since she herself acts only through vice – since everything, both in her will and in her works, is crime, corruption, vice and disorder?

'And from whom, other than her, do we receive those promptings which lead us into evil? Is it not her voice which whispers them to us? Are there any of our wishes or sensations which do not come from her? Can you then say it is reasonable for her to let us have – or stimulate our desires for – things which would be useless to her? If, then, vice serves her why should we wish to oppose it? By what right should we strive to destroy it, and by what means should we resist its voice? A little more philosophy in the world would soon put things to rights, making it clear to legislators and magistrates that these vices which they blame and punish with so much rigour sometimes have a much greater degree of utility that the virtues they preach yet never reward.'

'But were I weak enough to accept this frightful system, Madame,' I replied to this woman who wished to corrupt me, 'how would you teach me to stifle the remorse which would spring up, instant by instant, in my heart?'

'Remorse is a chimera, Sophie,' answered Dubois. 'It is nothing but the imbecile murmur of a soul so weak that it dare not kill its own imaginings.'

'Is it possible to kill it?'

'Nothing could be easier! Repentance is an emotion one only feels for actions to which one is unaccustomed. If you repeat frequently enough those things which bring you remorse, you will finally extinguish it. Oppose it with the torch of the passions, with the powerful laws of self-interest – then it will quickly disappear. Remorse does not prove anything to be a crime. It merely indicates an easily subjugated soul. If some authority should present you with an absurd order that for the moment you were not to leave this room, you would not leave it without feelings of remorse however certain you were that there would be no evil in doing so.

'It is, therefore, untrue that remorse is caused only by crime. By convincing oneself of the nullity of crime, of its necessity in the general plan of nature, it becomes a simple enough thing to vanquish the remorse one might feel in committing it – just as simple as it would be to stifle the guilt you might feel were you to leave this room after receiving an unjustifiable order to remain in it. It is necessary to begin with an exact analysis of that which men call crime, convincing oneself from the start that it is only the infringement of national laws and customs that is meant. What is defined as crime in France ceases to be such a few hundred miles away. There is no action universally considered as a crime over the whole face of the earth. Consequently nothing, at bottom, reasonably merits the name of crime. It is all just a matter of geography and opinion.

'With that much admitted, it becomes absurd to want to submit oneself to the practice of virtues which elsewhere are vices, and to flee from criminal actions which, in another climate, are esteemed as virtues. Consider carefully what I have said and then let me ask you if a man who – either for pleasure or interest – performs in France one of the virtues of China or Japan (but which in his own country is looked upon as a dishonourable act) should feel any remorse? Should he allow this vile distinction to prevent his action? And if he has a little philosophy in his spirit, will it be capable of making him feel remorse? But if remorse exists only as a form of prohibition, is born only from the overthrow of restraint – and not at all from the action in itself – is it truly wise to permit such an emotion to thrive within oneself? Isn't it absurd not to stamp it out immediately?

'A man should accustom himself to looking with indifference upon those actions which have caused him remorse. He should judge them only by way of an intensive study of the manners and customs of all the nations in the world. Subsequently he should repeat such actions as often as possible – whatever they may be – and the bright flame of reason will quickly destroy any lingering of remorse. It will annihilate this tenebrous influence which is merely the fruit of ignorance, pusillanimity, and education.

'For thirty years, Sophie, a perpetual indulgence in vice and crime has led me step by step towards fortune. I'm touching it now! Another two or three lucky shots and I shall have left far behind me that miserable state of mendacity into which I was born, replacing it by an income of more than fifty thousand livres. Do you imagine that, throughout a career which I have pursued with brilliance, remorse has even for a single moment made me feel the prick of its thorns? Don't believe such a thing is possible with me, for I have never known it! Within an instant some frightful reverse might suddenly plunge me from the pinnacle into the abyss – yet I would never admit it! I would blame either other people or my own clumsiness, but I would always be at peace with my conscience . . .'

'That may be,' I replied. 'But let me reason with you for a moment upon these same philosophical principles. By what right do you pretend to claim that my own conscience should be as strong as yours, since it has not been accustomed from childhood to vanquishing similar prejudices? By what virtue do you demand that my spirit, organised differently from your own, should be able to adopt the same systems? You admit that there are equal quantities of good and evil in nature, and that consequently there must be a certain number of beings practising the one with a second class of persons devoted to the other. The part which I play, even according to your own reasoning, is thus quite within the bounds of nature. I must therefore ask you not to insist that I depart from those rules which nature has laid down for me; for just as you find happiness in the career you follow, it would be equally impossible for me to find it outside my own special path. Besides, you must not imagine that the vigilance of the law leaves transgressors untouched for any length of time. Haven't you just seen such an example with your very eyes? Don't you remember the fifteen criminals with whom I had the misfortune to live? One is saved and fourteen perish ignominiously!'

'Is that what you would call misfortune? Anyway, what does this ignominy mean to an individual without principles? When one has left everything behind, when honour has become nought but a prejudice, reputation a chimera, and the future an illusion, isn't it a matter of indifference whether one dies in prison, or on one's bed at home?

There are two species of criminal in this world. One, backed by a powerful fortune and prodigious influence, can escape a tragic end. The other, if he is caught, will suffer. Yet, born with nothing, such a man must, if he is intelligent, have only two points of view: a fortune, or the wheel. If he manages to obtain the first then he has what he has always desired. If he is condemned to the second, what has he to regret since he has nothing to lose?

'It is for these reasons that the laws are powerless over criminals – they have, in fact, no existence for such men. The powerful and wealthy are able to escape the arm of the law; while the poor and unfortunate, having no choice but to live by their wits, cannot afford to be frightened by it!'

'Don't you believe that in the next world heaven's justice awaits those who have had the effrontery to indulge in crime on earth?'

'I believe that if there were a God there would be less evil on this earth. I also believe that if evil exists in our world then its disorders are necessitated by this God, or it is beyond his power to prevent them. But I can't be at all frightened of a God who is either weak or wicked. I defy him without any fear and laugh at his thunderings.'

'You make me tremble, Madame,' I said, as I rose to my feet. 'Forgive me if I cannot listen any longer to your execrable sophisms and your odious blasphemies!'

'Wait, Sophie; if I can't conquer your reasoning at least I may be able to tempt the feelings of your heart. I need you, therefore don't refuse me your help. Here are a hundred louis. Under your very eyes I lay them aside. They belong to you, as soon as the blow is struck!'

Listening to nothing but my natural tendency towards goodness, I asked la Dubois what this was all about – so that, with everything in my power, I might prevent whatever crime she was intending to commit.

'Here we are, then,' she said. 'Have you noticed the young merchant from Lyons who has been eating with us for the past three days?'

'Who? – Dubreuil?'

'Precisely!'

'What of it?'

'He is in love with you, and confided the fact to me. He has six hundred thousand francs, either in gold or on paper, which he keeps in a very small box near his bed. Let me lead this man to believe that you will consent to listen to him. It doesn't matter to you whether it is true or not! I'll suggest that he asks you to go for a stroll with him in some pleasant spot outside the town, implying that this will give him an excellent opportunity to increase his chances with you. It'll be up to you to amuse him, and keep him away from here as long as possible. In the meanwhile I shall rob him, but I shan't run away. His belongings will be sent to Turin but I shall remain in Grenoble.

'We shall employ every possible means to divert his suspicions, going even as far as helping him try to find the culprits. Then I shall announce my departure, which won't surprise him in the least; after which you can follow me and your hundred louis will be handed to you in Piedmont.'

'Yes, I'll do it, Madame,' I said to la Dubois, quite determined to warn the unfortunate Dubreuil of the infamous trick she was about to play on him.

And, the better to deceive this vicious woman, I added: 'Madame, you should reflect well on the fact that if Dubreuil is in love with me, I can extract from him much more money than you offer me – simply by warning him of your intentions or selling myself to him!'

'That is true,' answered Dubois. 'Honestly, I'm beginning to believe that heaven had blessed you with an even greater perspicacity in crime than my own. Ah, well,' she continued as she wrote, ' – here is my note for a thousand louis. Refuse me now, if you dare!'

'Under the circumstances, certainly not, Madame!' I said as I accepted the bill. 'But you must attribute my error in making this agreement only to my unfortunate condition, to my weakness of will, and to the need I feel for returning the help you once gave me.'

'I wanted to compliment you on your intelligence,' answered Dubois, 'but I see that you prefer me to accuse your misfortune. It shall be as you wish. Serve me always and you shall be content!'

Everything was arranged; and that same evening I commenced to make a little play at Dubreuil, realising immediately that he had some liking for me.

Nothing could have been more embarrassing than such a situation. I had no intention whatever of lending myself to the proposed crime, even had there been three times the amount of money in it for me. Yet I was utterly revolted by the thought of sending to the gallows a woman who, ten years previously, had gained me my liberty. I wanted to prevent the crime without the necessity of denouncing her. And had I been dealing with any but such an accomplished criminal as la Dubois I would surely have succeeded. Such was my aim; but I was unaware that the crafty manoeuvres of this abominable creature not only would cause the entire edifice of my honest intentions to crumble, but would also punish me for having conceived them.

On the day set apart for the intended rendezvous la Dubois invited us both to dine in her private room. We accepted, and when the meal was over Dubreuil and I descended to hasten the preparation of the carriage which we had ordered. As she did not accompany us I found myself alone for an instant with my escort.

'Monsieur,' I said precipitately, 'listen to me very carefully – don't attract any attention, whatever you do; and above all follow my instructions rigorously! Have you a friend at this inn?'

'Yes, I have a young associate whom I can trust as though he were myself . . . '

'Well, Monsieur, go quickly and tell him not to leave your room for a moment while we are away!'

'But I have locked my room and have the key in my pocket! Why this additional precaution?'

'It is much more essential than you may think, Monsieur! Please do as I say, or I shall not go with you. The woman whose room we have just left is one of the most vicious of criminals. It was she who engineered this outing in order that she might rob you the more easily. Hurry, Monsieur – she is watching us, and she is most dangerous. She mustn't guess that I have said anything to you. Give your key immediately to your friend, telling him to wait for us in your room with some companions if this is possible. And it is important that they must stay there, never leaving the place vacant, until we return. I will explain the why and the wherefore as soon as we are in the carriage . . . '

Dubreuil listened to me, pressing my hand with gratitude. Then he ran back to the inn to carry out my suggestions. When he returned we set off in our carriage and I was able to explain the entire situation to him. The young man pledged me every possible gratitude for the service I had rendered him. Then, having obliged me to tell him the truth concerning my situation, he swore that nothing he had learned of my adventures would deter him from offering me both his hand and his fortune.

'Our rank is equal,' Dubreuil said to me. 'I am a merchant's son, just as you are a merchant's daughter. My business has proved very successful, but your life has been most unfortunate. I should therefore be more than happy if I could make amends to you for the wrongs which fate has brought you. Consider my proposal carefully, Sophie! I am my own master and depend on no one else. I am on my way to Geneva, where I shall make considerable investments with those sums which your thoughtful warning has enabled me to save from thieving hands. You must follow me there, and on your arrival I shall become your husband. Thenceforward you will appear in Lyons only as my wife.'

Such a delightful experience flattered me so much that I dared not even consider refusing it. Yet it was scarcely seemly to accept without first acquainting Dubreuil with matters which might later cause him regret. He was more than pleased with my honesty, pressing me more insistently than ever to marry him . . . Unfortunate creature that I was; it seemed that whenever happiness was offered me I should feel only more vividly the pain caused by my inability to seize it. It seemed, indeed, one of providence's unwritten yet most definite decrees, that never should a virtue open its buds within my heart without precipitating me into suffering and wretchedness! Our conversation had already taken us more than two miles out of town, and we were about to alight from the carriage to enjoy the freshness of a walk through some of those beautiful green alleys which grace the banks of the Isèhe – when suddenly Dubreuil told me that he felt terribly ill . . . As soon as we had left our seats he was seized with the most frightful attack of vomiting. Immediately I made him get back into the carriage and we returned at the utmost speed towards Grenoble. The young man was so desperately ill that he had to be carried up to his room. The state he was in absolutely astonished his friends who, following his orders, had never left his apartment. I didn't leave him for a moment . . . A doctor arrived and, merciful heaven, when the diagnosis had been made it was found that Dubreuil had been poisoned . . . Scarcely did I learn this dreadful news than I flew to the room of la Dubois . . . The vicious creature had gone . . . Running to my own room I found my wardrobe had been forced open and what little money and clothing I possessed had been stolen; la Dubois, I was informed, had departed three hours earlier having boarded the stage to Turin . . .

There could be no doubt whatever but that she was the author of this multitude of crimes. She had gone to the young man's room and, enraged at finding it occupied by his friends, had avenged herself upon me. She had poisoned Dubreuil during the dinner so that, had she succeeded in her schemes, he being much more concerned with the saving of his life than with pursuing her, she would be able to escape in safety. Moreover, as he would almost certainly die – so to speak – in my arms, I would be much more open to suspicion than herself. I quickly ran back to Dubreuil but was not allowed to approach him. He expired, surrounded by his friends, completely exonerating me and assuring them of my innocence. He forbade them, above all, to involve me in any prosecution. Hardly had he closed his eyes than his associate hastened to bring me this news, assuring me that I had no reason to be disturbed . . .

Alas, how could I refrain from weeping bitterly at the loss of the only man who, since the commencement of my misfortunes, had so generously offered to lift me out of them! . . . How could I cease deploring a theft which plunged me back into that fatal abyss of misery from which it seemed that I should never be able to extricate myself? I confided everything to Dubreuil's business associate, telling him all about the plot against his friend and then all that had been done to myself. He sympathised with me deeply, bitterly regretting the death of his friend and criticising the excess of delicacy which had prevented me from lodging an immediate complaint against la Dubois once I had learned the details of her project. We were perfectly aware that this horrible creature, who needed but four hours to be in safety, would already have reached her destination before we could arrange the details for her pursuit. Such a pursuit would certainly have been costly; and the inn keeper, doubtless much compromised by the complaints I might lodge, would most certainly have made a considerable noise in his own defence – which might perhaps have resulted in crushing completely a person known in Grenoble only as someone discharged after a criminal trial and relying entirely upon public charity for her subsistence . . .

These reasons so convinced and terrified me that I resolved to leave without saying goodbye to Monsieur S—, my protector. Dubreuil's friend fully approved of my leaving in this way, and he made no attempt to hide from me the fact that, should the adventure come to light, the depositions he would necessarily have to make would undoubtedly compromise me, whatever precautions he took – just as much because of my relationship with la Dubois as because of my drive with his friend. So it was natural that he should urge me to leave Grenoble immediately without seeing anyone, assuring me, for his own part, that he would never instigate any form of action against me.

Meditating in private on the entire affair, I was obliged to admit to myself that the young man's advice was especially pertinent, for it was quite certain that I looked just as guilty as I was actually innocent. For the only thing which might be cited in my favour – the warning I had given Dubreuil, incompletely explained by him as he was dying – was perhaps not so incontrovertible a proof as I had hoped. It did not take me long to make my decision and I quickly communicated it to Dubreuil's associate.

'I only wish,' he said, 'that my friend had instructed me to make some arrangements which would really be helpful for you. Had he done so I would have carried them out with the deepest pleasure. I also wish he had been able to tell me that it was due to your intervention that he placed a guard in his room while out on his excursion with you. But he wasn't able to do so. He only repeated over and over again that you were completely innocent and that we must avoid prosecuting you in any way whatsoever.

'I am therefore obliged to confine myself to carrying out such orders as he left. The losses you have suffered in helping him suggest that I should do something myself to help you, Madamoiselle. But I am just starting my own business, and as I am young my finances are extremely limited. Not a sou of Dubreuil's money belonged to me and I am obliged to return it all to his family. Nevertheless, Sophie, perhaps you will permit me to do the best I can for you, however small the amount. Here are five louis – and here,' he said, calling into the room a woman whom I had noticed previously in the inn, ' – here is an honest shop keeper from my own town – Chalon-sur-Saône. She is returning home after a day spent in Lyons on business.'

'Madame Bertrand,' said the young man as he presented her to me, 'here is a young lady whom I recommend to your protection. She would very much like to find work in the country; and I beg you, as though you were my agent in the matter, to do everything in your power to find her a suitable place in our town – one befitting her birth and education. Do not request anything of her until this has been done. I shall take care of everything next time I see you . . . Until then, goodbye, Sophie . . . Madame Bertrand is leaving tonight. Go with her, and may good luck follow you in a town where I shall soon, I hope, have the pleasure of seeing you again – and of proving to you, for the remainder of my life, the gratitude I feel for the sincerity of your behaviour with Dubreuil.'

The kindness of this young man, who really owed me nothing, caused me, despite myself, to start weeping. I accepted his gifts gladly, swearing to him that I should work only for that day when I would be able to repay his gestures. 'Alas,' I said to myself as I left him, 'if the exercise of another virtue has precipitated me once more into misfortune, at least – and for the first time in my life – a little consolation has been offered me in this terrifying chasm of evil wherein virtue herself has thrown me.' I did not see my young benefactor again, and I left, as had been arranged with la Bertrand on the night after Dubreuil's unfortunate end.

La Bertrand has a little covered carriage drawn by a horse, and we took turns in driving it from inside. Therein were her belongings, together with a reasonable sum of money and a little girl of eighteen months whom she was still nursing. I became equally as much attached to this child as was the mother who had given her life.

Madame Bertrand was a kind of fish-wife, as deficient in education as she was in intelligence. She was suspicious, gossiping, boring, and narrow-minded – as almost all working-class women seem to be. Every evening we removed all her goods from the little carriage, took them into whatever inn we happened to be staying at and kept them with us in our room while we slept. Nothing extraordinary occurred until we arrived in Lyons, but on one of the two days which this women needed for her business there I experienced a very singular encounter. I was walking along the quay which borders the Rhône, accompanied by one of the girls from the inn – whom I had asked to accompany me – when suddenly I saw coming towards us the Reverend Father Antonin, butcher of my virginity, now one of the Superiors of this city and, as you will remember, known so well to me when my unfortunate star led me to the little monastery of Sainte-Marie-des-Bois. He accosted me in cavalier fashion, asking me in front of the servant-girl if I wouldn't like to come and see him in his new residence, there to indulge once more our former pleasures.

Such a conversation made me blush prodigiously, and for a moment I tried to make him think he had mistaken my identity. Not succeeding, however, I attempted to convey to him by signs that he ought at least to contain himself in front of my guide. But nothing affected this insolent creature and his solicitations only became the more pressing. At length, on our repeated refusals to follow him, he contented himself with asking for our address. In order to get rid of him I gave him a false one. Noting it down in his pocket-book he left us, assuring us that we should be seeing him very soon.

The girl and I retraced our steps. On our way I did my best to explain to her the story of this unfortunate acquaintance, but whether my words proved unsatisfactory, or perhaps because of the girl's natural need to chatter, I later realised from certain words of la Bertrand – uttered at the time of the dreadful adventure which was to befall me with her – that she had been informed of my acquaintance with this villainous monk. Nevertheless, we did not see him again and shortly afterwards left the city. Departing from Lyons late that day, we did not reach Villefranche until evening. And it was there, Madame, that I met with the horrible catastrophe which, today, must make me seem a criminal in your eyes. Yet I remain no more a criminal in this present disastrous situation than I was in those which I have already related to you. Nothing but the sentiment of kindness – which I have never been able to extinguish from my heart – has led me to this abyss of misfortune, this repeated suffering under the unjust blows of fate.

It was six o'clock one February evening when we arrived at Villefranche, where we took a hurried supper, retiring early to bed so that we might cover even more ground on the following day. We hadn't been asleep more than two hours when frightful clouds of smoke began to fill our room, immediately arousing each of us with a

start! We couldn't possibly doubt but that the fire was nearby . . .
Merciful heaven! – its progress was already terrifying. Almost naked,
we opened our door, hearing nothing but the crash of tumbling walls,
the frightful noise of splitting timbers, and the blood-curdling howls of
the unlucky wretches who fell into that blazing inferno. Countless
tongues of these devouring flames lashed towards us, scarcely leaving
us time to throw ourselves into the street. We found ourselves in the
midst of a crowd of unfortunates who, naked as ourselves and some of
them half-roasted, had sought their safety in flight . . .

It was at that moment I remembered that Madame Bertrand, more
concerned with saving her own life than with snatching her daughter
from death, had left the child behind. Without a word to her I flew
through the flames and up to our room. Blinded and burned as I was I
seized the poor little creature and ran to hand her to her mother.
Leaning for a moment against a half-consumed beam I lost my footing
and automatically stretched out my hand to save myself. This natural
movement caused me to drop the precious bundle I was holding and
the unfortunate little girl fell into the flames under her mother's very
eyes! The terrible woman, thinking neither of my attempt to save her
child nor of the state in which my fall had left me, but carried away by
the delirium and pain of her loss, accused me of the death of her
daughter and, impetuously throwing herself on top of me, overwhelmed me with her blows.

Meanwhile the course of the fire was arrested, concerted labour
having saved almost half of the inn. Madame Bertrand's first care was
to return to her room, which happened to be one of those least
damaged. She renewed her complaints, telling me I should have left
her daughter where she was, for then she would not have risked
danger. But you can imagine what happened to her when, looking for
her possessions, she found that they had all been stolen! Her rage and
her despair were terrible to hear, and she openly accused me of having
caused the fire purposely so that I might rob her with greater ease. She
told me she was going to denounce me and very quickly put her threat
into effect by asking to speak to the local judge.

Well might I protest my innocence; yet she wouldn't listen to a word!
The magistrate was not far away, for it was he who had ordered and
organised the fighting of the fire, and he appeared almost immediately
on the request of this wicked woman . . . She lodged her complaint
against me, supporting it with every piece of evidence she could think
of, and, describing me as a girl of loose morals who had escaped the
hangman's rope at Grenoble, said that my company had been forced on
her by a young man whose mistress I must doubtless be. She spoke of

the monk at Lyons, and forgot no calumny which might be suggested by a vengeance fostered by despair and poisoned with rage.

The judge received her complaint. The house was examined and it was discovered that the blaze had commenced in a storehouse filled with hay. Several people testified that they had seen me going into it that evening, which was true. For, looking for a lavatory and being carelessly directed by the servants, I had wandered into this place, staying long enough to arouse suspicion. Thus the proceedings began, and were followed according to the strictest rule. The witnesses were heard but nothing I could say in my defence was ever listened to. It was shown that I must be the incendiary and proved that I had accomplices who, while I was at one end of the house, committed their theft at the other. Without being enlightened further I was taken at dawn next day to the prison at Lyons, where I was registered as an incendiary, child-murderer, and thief.

Being so long accustomed to slander, injustice, and misfortune – having felt from very childhood the thorns in every virtuous emotion – my pain was a dull stupefaction rather than an agonised rending, and I wept more than I complained. Nevertheless, as it is natural enough for a suffering creature to seek every means possible to extricate themselves from the abyss into which fate has plunged them, I could scarcely avoid letting the thought of Father Antonin enter my mind. However little help I might expect of him, I could not avoid a desire to see him, and therefore asked for him. As he did not know I had requested him, he appeared, affecting, nevertheless, not to recognise me. Then I told the concierge that he possibly didn't remember me, having directed my conscience when I was very young. On the strength of this I requested a private interview with him, which was granted. As soon as I was alone with the monk I threw myself at his feet and begged him to save me from the cruel position in which I found myself. I proved my innocence to him, nor did I hide from him the fact that his disgusting propositions of two days previously had completely destroyed my reputation in the eyes of the woman to whom I had been recommended.

The monk listened to me with considerable attention and scarcely had I finished when he said: 'Listen to me, Sophie, and don't comport yourself as you ordinarily do as soon as someone infringes your accursed prejudices. You see where your principles have led you. Now you have plenty of time in which to convince yourself that they have never served any other purpose than to plunge you from one abyss into another. Cease from following them one step further if you wish to save your life. As for that, I see only one method that will succeed. We have with us a Father who is closely related both to the Governor and to the Prison Commissioner. I shall inform him concerning the facts. You must say that you are his niece, then by reclaiming you as such and giving his promise that you will remain in a convent for life, we will almost certainly be able to prevent proceedings from progressing further. You will disappear. He will place you in my care and I shall undertake the responsibility of hiding you until suitable circumstances permit me to restore you to liberty But you will be entirely mine during this detention. I am not attempting to hide the fact from you. You will submit yourself absolutely to my caprices, abandoning yourself utterly to their gratification. You understand what that means, Sophie? – You know me, and you have your choice between this and the scaffold. I shan't wait for your answer!'

'Go away, Father!' I replied with horror. 'Go away! You are a monster so cruelly to abuse my situation, and to give me only the choice between death and infamy! Leave me here. I would rather die innocently, for then at least I should die without remorse!'

My resistance inflamed this traitorous wretch. He dared to show me the point to which his passion had been stimulated. The infamous lecher had dared to picture the caresses of love within the horror of the prison with its chains – beneath the very blade which was waiting to lay me low. I tried to escape him but he caught me, tumbling me over on the miserable straw which served as my bed. And if he did not entirely consummate his crime, at least he covered me with such revolting stains that it was impossible for me to doubt his abominable designs.

'Listen,' he said to me as he readjusted his habit. 'You don't want me to help you, so I'm going to abandon you. I shan't serve you, nor shall I hurt you in any way. But if you decide to say a single word against me, I shall charge you with the most enormous crimes and thus remove all possibility of your defending yourself. Reflect well on what I have said before you speak, and grasp the spirit of what I am about to say to the gaoler or I'll do away with you this very instant.'

He gave a knock and the concierge entered.

'Monsieur,' said this vicious monk, 'this good young woman is mistaken. She really wanted to speak with a Father Antonin from Bordeaux. I neither know him, nor have I ever heard of him. But she has asked me to hear her confession and I have done so. You are aware of our regulations – therefore I have nothing more to say. I bid you both good-day, and shall always be ready to present myself here when my ministrations shall be deemed necessary.'

Antonin left as he said these words, and I was as stupefied by his deceit as I was confounded by his insolence and lust.

The lower tribunals act very quickly. They are nearly always

composed of idiots, of imbeciles and brutal fanatics of men who are
sure that wiser and better informed eyes will correct the stupidities
which they regularly commit. Thus was I unanimously condemned to
death by eight or ten jumped-up little men who composed the
respectable tribunal of this town of bankrupts. I was immediately sent
to Paris for confirmation of my sentence. It was then that the most sad
and bitter of thoughts began to assail and tear at my heart.

'Under what fatal star was it necessary that I should be born?' I
murmured to myself. 'Why is it impossible for me to feel even a single
virtuous sentiment without its promptly being followed by a deluge of
trouble and suffering? And how can it be that this radiant providence,
whose justice I have been pleased to adore, has not only punished me
for my virtues but has, at the same time, raised to the very pinnacle of
success those very people who have crushed me with their vices?
During my childhood a money-lender tried to persuade me to steal. I
refused him, but he grew rich and I was almost hanged. Some
scoundrels would have raped me in a wood because I refused to join
their gang. They prospered, but as for myself, I fell into the hands of a
debauched Marquis who gave me a hundred strokes of the lash because
I did not wish to poison his mother. After that a surgeon whom I
prevented from committing an abominable crime, rewarded my efforts
by mutilating me, branding me, and kicking me out on the street.
Though doubtless he committed other crimes, he made his fortune
while I was forced to beg for bread. I wanted to draw near to the Holy
Sacraments, fervently to implore the Supreme Being for His help. The
sacred building where I had hoped to purify myself in one of our most
holy mysteries became the terrifying theatre of my dishonour and
ignominy. The monster who abused and polluted me was raised
instantly to the highest honour, whilst I was cast back into the frightful
abyss of my misery. I wanted to help a poor man, but he robbed me. I
would have given help to a wounded and almost unconscious man, but
the traitor made me turn a wheel like any beast of burden. He rained
blows on me when my strength failed. Yet every possible favour was
heaped on him – while I nearly lost my life because I had been forced
into working for him. A worthless woman attempted to coax me into
fresh crimes. Once more I lost the little I possessed in an attempt to
save the fortune of her victim and preserve him from suffering. This
young man would have rewarded me by giving me his hand in
marriage – but he died in my arms. I exposed myself to considerable
risk in a fire to save another woman's child – and here I am for the third
time underneath the blade of Themis. Imploring the protection of a
wretch who prostituted me, I had hoped to find him sensitive to my

endless suffering. But the barbarian only offered his assistance at the
price of renewed dishonour . . . Oh, providence, has the possibility of
doubting your justice finally been granted me? Could I have been
afflicted by any greater scourges, had I, like my persecutors, always
worshipped at the altars of vice?'

Such, Madame, were the blasphemies which, in spite of myself, I dared
allow to pass my lips . . . They were torn from me by the horror of my
fate. And then you deigned to let fall on me a glance filled with pity and
compassion . . . I offer you a thousand apologies, Madame, for having
so long abused your patience. I have reopened my wounds, I have
troubled your repose – and that is the most either of us has gained from
the recital of my cruel adventures. The morning star is high and my
guards will shortly come to take me away. Let me run to meet death. I
fear her no longer. She will cut short my torments for she will finish
them completely. She is only to be feared by those fortunate beings
whose days are filled with purity and serenity. But the unfortunate
creature who has trodden only upon adders, whose bleeding feet have
encountered little but thorns, who has known men only to hate them,
and who has seen dawn light the sky only to detest it – she who has
known the loss of parents, fortune, help, protection, friends, who has
tears for her drink and tribulation for her nourishment – such an one, I
say, is able to watch the approach of death without a shudder, wishing
for it as a haven of safety where she will experience the rebirth of
tranquillity in the bosom of a God who is too just to permit an
innocence, humiliated and persecuted on earth, not to find in heaven
the full reward of its tears.

❧ *Five* ❧

The honest Monsieur de Corville had been deeply moved as he listened to this story. As for Madame de Lorsange (the monstrous errors of whose youth had not – as we have already said – entirely extinguished all sensitivity in her heart), she was on the point of fainting.

'Mademoiselle,' she said to Sophie. 'It is impossible to listen to you without being profoundly interested in your case . . . But I must admit to you that an inexplicable feeling, even stronger than interest, draws me invincibly towards you and makes me feel your sufferings as though they were my own. You have not told me your name, Sophie, and you have concealed the details of your birth. I must beg you to unbare your secret before me. Please do not think that it is merely vain curiosity that causes me to speak thus. If what I suspect is true . . . Oh, Justine, if you were my sister!'

'Justine, Madame? . . . What a name!'

'She would be your age today!'

'Oh, Juliette, is it you that I hear!' exclaimed the unhappy prisoner as she threw herself into the arms of Madame de Lorsange . . . 'You, my sister, merciful God . . . What blasphemy have I uttered? I have even doubted providence! . . . Ah, I shall die infinitely less miserably since I have been permitted to embrace you once again!'

And the two sisters, closely pressed in each other's arms, expressed themselves to each other only in sobs, spoke only in tears . . . Monsieur de Corville could not restrain his own; and seeing that it would be quite impossible for him not to take the greatest interest in this affair, he immediately retired to his study.

There he wrote to the Keeper of the Seals, painting in strokes of blood the terrible fate of the unfortunate Justine. He guaranteed her innocence, begging, until she could be retried, that her only prison should be his château; and he pledged himself as her representative before the Supreme Officer of Justice. As soon as the letter was written he handed it to two cavaliers of the guard, ordering them to deliver it immediately and to return to his house for their prisoner should the

Chief of the Magistrature demand it. These two men, seeing with whom they were dealing, had no fear of compromising themselves in obeying his orders. Meanwhile a carriage had drawn up. .

'Come, beautiful but unfortunate creature,' said Monsieur de Corville to Justine, ' – come! Everything has changed for you in the past quarter of an hour. Never shall it be said that your virtue did not find its reward here below, or that you never met with any hearts but those fashioned from steel . . . Follow me! You are my prisoner now, and no one other than myself shall answer for you!'

Then in a few words he explained what he had done . . .

'You wonderful man! You are as generous as you are influential!' exclaimed Madame de Lorsange, as she threw herself at her lover's knees. 'This is the most magnificent act you have ever performed. And it is for you, who truly know the heart of mankind and the spirit of the law, to avenge persecuted innocence, to help those who are overwhelmed by fate . . . Go, Justine, go! . . . run immediately to kiss the feet of this equitable protector, who will never abandon you as the others have done! Oh, Monsieur, if our love was previously precious to me, how much more so is it now, embellished by the knots of nature and closely tied by the most tender affection!'

And the two women struggled with each other to clasp the knees of so generous a friend, watering them with their tears. Monsieur de Corville and Madame de Lorsange took the keenest delight in taking Justine from the excessive hardships of her previous life to the very heights of prosperity and luxury. Delightedly they fed her on the most succulent of dishes, gave her the softest of beds, and presented her with complete freedom of command over all they owned. In all this they manifested the extreme delicacy which one expects in two such sensitive souls . . . They supplied her with medicinal remedies for several days, bathed her, dressed her, and adorned her exquisitely. Both of these two lovers adored her. They even competed with each other as to who would first be successful in causing her to forget her misfortunes. A specialist was called in so that he might, with skilled treatment, remove the ignominious mark which Rodin had left upon her. Everything succeeded according to the wishes of Madame de Lorsange and her intelligent lover. Already the traces of misfortune were effaced from the charming brow of the amiable Justine . . . Already the graces were re-establishing their empire over her. To the livid tint of her alabaster cheeks succeeded the roses of springtime. And laughter, absent so long from those lips, reappeared at last, borne on the wings of pleasure.

Soon the most wonderful news arrived from Paris. Monsieur de Corville had agitated the whole of France, reviving the zeal of Monsieur S—, who joined hands with him in painting the sufferings of Justine; and together they did their utmost to bring to her that tranquillity she so much deserved. Eventually letters arrived from the King himself clearing the young woman completely of every charge and of all proceedings brought against her since childhood. He restored her to her rightful position as an honest citizen, imposing a permanent and enduring silence upon every court in the country that had conspired against her. Above and beyond all this he granted her an annuity of twelve hundred livres to be derived from the funds seized in the workshop of the counterfeiters of Dauphiné. When she heard such agreeable news Justine almost fainted with delight. During several days she shed the sweetest of tears over the breasts of her protectors; until, quite suddenly, her mood changed, without anyone being able to divine the cause. She became melancholy, disquieted, dreamy, and sometimes wept before her friends, without even being able to explain the cause of her tears.

'I was not born for such a full measure of happiness,' she often said to Madame de Lorsange . . . 'Oh, my dear sister, it is impossible for such joy to last!'

Every attempt had been made to prove to her that her sufferings were over, that she no longer had the slightest cause for anxiety. It was pointed out what meticulous care had been exercised in drawing up the official reports on her case, and how none of the individuals with whom she had been compromised had ever been named – thus removing any possibility of danger from their influence. Yet she remained inconsolable. Nothing could quiet her; and anyone observing her might have said that this poor girl, uniquely destined to experience misfortune and always sensing the hand of fate suspended above her head, already foresaw the final blow which was about to crush her.

Madame de Lorsange was still living in the country at this time. It was near the end of summer and an out-door excursion had been planned when a frightful storm broke loose. The excessive heat had obliged the inmates of the house to leave all the drawing-room windows wide open. The lightning flashed, the hail-stones fell, the wind blustered violently, and horrifying claps of thunder reverberated across the heavens . . . Madame de Lorsange, who was terrified of thunder, begged her sister to close the windows as quickly as she could. Monsieur de Corville entered the room just as she made this request; and Justine, anxious to calm her sister, flew to the windows, trying for a moment to fight against the wind which pushed her back.

At that instant a tongue of lightning, streaking into the room with a noisy crash, threw her backwards in her own steps and left her lifeless on the floor.

A lamentable shriek escaped from Madame de Lorsange . . . and then she fainted. Monsieur de Corville called for help, dividing the attentions of his domestics equally between the two sisters. Madame de Lorsange was quickly brought back to consciousness but the unfortunate Justine had been struck in such a fashion as left no hope for her. The lightning had entered by her right breast, consuming her bosom; and, leaving by her mouth, had so disfigured her features that she was horrible to look on. Monsieur de Corville wished to have the body removed immediately, but Madame de Lorsange, rising to her feet with the utmost calm, firmly opposed him.

'No,' she said to her lover. 'No! Leave her there where I can see her for a little while. I have need to contemplate her in order to strengthen myself in a resolution I have just made. Listen to me, Monsieur, and do not attempt to oppose in any way the course I am about to adopt, and from which nothing in the world can now dissuade me!

'The unheard of misfortunes experienced by this unhappy girl – despite the fact that she worshipped virtue above all – contain within themselves something so extraordinary, Monsieur, that they have opened my eyes on my own life. Do not imagine that I am blinded by the false gleams of felicity which, during the course of her adventures, we have seen enjoyed by the treacherous individuals who tormented her. Such caprices of fate are the enigmas of providence which we should not unveil and by which we must never allow ourselves to be seduced. The prosperity of the wicked is simply one of the means by which the Almighty proves our strength. It is like the lightning, the deceptive fires of which only illuminate the atmosphere for a moment so as to precipitate its unfortunate victim into the abyss of death . . . Here, before our eyes, is the very example! The uninterrupted calamities and terrible sufferings of this unfortunate girl are a warning sent to me by the Eternal, asking me to repent my irregular way of life, to listen to the voice of my remorse, and to throw myself at last into His arms. What dreadful treatment must I fear from Him! I, whose crimes would make you shudder were they known to you! . . . I, who have been marked at every step in my life by libertinism, irreligion and the absence of those principles I so prodigally discarded . . . What can I expect when she who is without sin – who had not a single crime with which to reproach her days – is treated thus?

'We must part, Monsieur, for I still have time . . . We are not tied by any legal bond. Forget me, and know that it is good and fitting thing that I go to repent eternally, abjuring at the feet of the Almighty all those infamies with which I am soiled. Sad as it may be, this frightful blow was nevertheless necessary to my conversion in this life and to that happiness for which I dare to hope in the life to come. Adieu, Monsieur, you will never see me again. As a final token of your friendship I beg that you will refrain from any sort of enquiry into what has become of me. I shall await you in a better world, where your virtues must assuredly conduct you. May the mortifications I shall undertake to expiate my crimes allow me, when my miserable years are over, to see you there again one day.'

Madame de Lorsange ordered a carriage to be got ready and left the house immediately. Taking a sum of money with her, she left all the remainder to be disposed of by Monsieur de Corville in pious donations. As quickly as possibly she sped to Paris, where she entered a Carmelite Convent; wherein, after very few years, she became the model and example, as much by her great piety as by her wisdom, her intelligence and the moral perfection of her behaviour.

Monsieur de Corville, having long been worthy of the highest positions his country could offer, attained them at last. And from his honoured position worked for the happiness of the people, the glory of his sovereign and the fortune of his friends.

Oh you who read this story, may you draw from it the same profit as that worldly woman whom Heaven finally corrected. May you be convinced, with her, that true happiness is only to be found in the bosom of virtue, and that if God permits it to be persecuted here on earth, it is only to prepare for it a more flattering reward in Heaven.

Completed, in fifteen days, on 8th July 1787

Wordsworth Classic Erotica